Stories From The Heart

Third Edition

by

Steve Demaree

Each of these stories is written to make you think. Some of them may make you laugh or cry, and I hope all of them make you want to share them with others.

2nd Hesitations Publishing

Third Edition Printing   August 2003

Additional copies of this book are available by mail. Send
$15.00, which includes postage (Kentucky residents add
an additional .90 sales tax) to:
Steve Demaree
1608 Summerhill Drive
Lexington, Kentucky 40515
(859)271-2416
moviesteve@rocketmail.com

This book is printed in the USA by
Morris Publishing
3212 East Highway 30
Kearney, Nebraska 68847
(800) 650-7888

This book is dedicated to the two people I love the most and whose love I deserve the least, my wife Nell and my daughter Kelly. May God continue to bless me with their presence in my life.

This book is also dedicated to the seven people who bought the most copies of my first three books.

Les Aldrich, Washington, 40 copies

George Pettus, North Carolina, 26 copies

Allie (Bee) Calvert, Kentucky, 14 copies

Van Scott, Illinois, 13 copies

Chris Browning, Kentucky, 12 copies

Tim Miller, Kentucky, 11 copies

Nick Pyle, Virginia, 10 copies

My Thanks Also Goes Out To These People Who Helped Me With Editing And Proofreading This Book

Ken Kron, author of *Feet Of Clay*

Debby Perry

Tammy Morehead

Table Of Contents

Visitors Welcome

He was nameless and homeless, but he had not always been nameless and homeless. At one time he had been well-known, had a good job, and had a wife and two kids to come home to each evening. His world was ripped apart one night when a drunken driver rounded a curve in the wrong lane and took his family from him.

From then on he felt he had no reason to live. He quit his job and abandoned his home. He began to wander from place to place. He ate wherever he could find food and slept wherever his travels took him.

One evening he saw a notice on a storefront: WORSHIP SERVICE EVERY NIGHT THIS WEEK - DINNER SERVED - VISITORS WELCOME.

The church was nearby. It was the first night of the week-long worship services and he was hungry. He walked into the brisk wind and headed for the church. He went inside and waited until all the others had gone through the food line. When he got to the serving table tears fell from his eyes. He hurriedly filled his plate and went to a corner to eat.

After he ate he followed the others to the worship service where he found a seat on the back pew. Although he slid quietly into the pew, people noticed him. Everyone looked at the man who wore a raggedy coat and shoes with holes in them. Each person seemed to notice that he needed a shower and a shave.

The first night's sermon was about love, and he felt warm inside when he heard the congregation sing *Oh, How I Love Jesus*. When the service ended, he bowed his head for a moment and then got up to go back out into the cold.

The next night he came back and he brought a homeless friend. He enjoyed seeing his friend eat because he knew that his friend had had nothing to eat for two days.

7

As the two of them took a seat in the sanctuary, many of the congregation turned and looked at them and then whispered to a neighbor.

The pastor preached about The Good Samaritan, and the service closed with the singing of *Just As I Am*. As he started singing he felt a lump in his throat and tears began to stream down his cheeks. His friend noticed, too, and reached over and clasped his hand. When the service ended, he again bowed his head, only longer this time, and his friend did as well.

When he arrived at the church the following evening a man met him at the door.

"I'm sorry, my friend, but you cannot come in tonight. Some of the people of the church have complained."

"I don't understand. What did I do?" the homeless man asked.

"Some people look at you as a freeloader. I'm really sorry. If you promise not to come back, I'll fix you a sandwich. You can take it with you."

The homeless man felt like leaving, but he was hungry so he waited. Shortly, the man came back with a sandwich.

As the homeless man turned to leave, he looked up and saw his friend starting to climb the church steps.

"We aren't allowed in the church anymore. Here, take part of my sandwich."

His friend thanked him and turned to leave.

The homeless man stood reflecting as he watched his friend leave, and then headed off in the other direction.

He had gone only a few steps when he almost stumbled over something. As he glanced down, he noticed an old man with no legs huddled against the church to keep out of the wind.

"Hey, Mister! I'm really hungry. Could I have a bite of your sandwich?"

He bent over and gave the old man the rest of his sandwich and then he turned and walked away. As he turned to leave, the old man broke into a wide grin and hollered out to him, "Thank you, Jesus!"

The next night he found himself walking by another church with a sign that read: SERVICE TONIGHT - DINNER PROVIDED - VISITORS WELCOME, but he just walked on by into the night even though he was once again cold and hungry.

The Christmas Visitor

Martha looked out her window on a cold Christmas Eve morning. The snow had begun to taper off. She sat down in her rocker and began to reflect on having to spend another Christmas alone. Martha's daughter and son-in-law and their two children lived quite a distance from Martha, and she had no other family. Her daughter and grandchildren called regularly and they visited her each summer, but a call was not the same as a hug, a smile, and a face-to-face chat, and it was a long time until summer.

As Martha sat there rocking and thinking how few of her friends her age were still around, she fell asleep and began to dream. She dreamed that someone was knocking on her door.

As she opened the door she saw a man with a kindly face.

"May I shovel the snow from your walk?" the man asked.

"It depends on how much you charge. I'm on a fixed income," Martha replied.

"Oh, there will be no charge."

"No charge! You're kidding?"

"Oh, no ma'am."

"Well, how do you make any money?"

"Oh, I'm not doing this to make money, but to serve others."

"Well, I'll let you do it on one condition, and that's that you'll come in and have some hot chocolate and cookies after you finish."

"That sounds like a good deal to me," the man said as he set off to begin his work.

Since the snow was so deep, it took the stranger almost an hour to finish the job, but he did finish and he knocked on Martha's door to let her know that he was done.

Martha invited him in. She was so glad to have someone to talk to and share her cookies with that the two of them sat and talked for an hour.

"My family lives so far away, and I miss them dearly," Martha said to her visitor, "and I must tell you that I'm not looking forward to another Christmas alone. It's lonely here during the winter. I'm afraid to get out in the bad weather, and I hardly ever have visitors."

"I have a feeling that things will be different this year," the visitor replied.

Time passed quickly and eventually the visitor got up to leave.

"You don't know how much your stopping by has meant to me. I don't have to worry about finding someone to shovel my walk, and I really enjoyed getting to share my cookies with someone. Would you mind if I gave you a hug?"

"I'd love one," the stranger replied.

After they hugged, the stranger took hold of Martha's hands. As he let go, she noticed that his hands were scarred. She wanted to ask him what caused it but she decided not to ask.

Martha's visitor noticed her looking at his hands.

"It happened a long time ago when I was doing something for someone I loved," he told Martha.

Martha and the stranger hugged again and then he left.

A short time later Martha awakened to the chime of the doorbell. She wondered who it could be and hurried to the door. As she opened the door, she saw Sarah, the young woman who had recently moved in next door.

"Oh, hi, Sarah. What can I do for you today?"

"Actually Martha, it's more what I can do for you. Because of our jobs, Bill and I aren't going to be able to go home for Christmas, and we'd like for you to join us tomorrow if you don't have other plans."

"I'd love to! My daughter and son-in-law live too far away to come for Christmas, and to be honest with you, I wasn't looking forward to spending the day by myself."

"Great! Why don't you plan to come over for breakfast? Bill always fixes me a big breakfast for Christmas, and we'd love for you to enjoy it with us."

"That sounds wonderful! What time do you want me to come over?"

"Is 9:00 too early?"

"No, that would be great. I'm always up before 7:00. Would you like for me to bring anything?"

"No, this is our treat. See you in the morning."

As Sarah turned to leave, Martha noticed that her walk had been shoveled.

"By the way, Sarah, be sure and thank Bill for shoveling my walk."

"Oh, Bill didn't do it."

"He didn't! Do you have any idea who did?"

"He was a stranger to me, but he must've been someone familiar with the neighborhood, because the only two walks he shoveled were yours and Mrs. Parkington's. I guess he knew there was a man at all the other houses. Actually, that was what gave us the idea to invite you over."

Sarah and Martha said goodbye and Martha turned away from her door with a puzzled look on her face. Martha shut the door and went back to her rocker where she noticed on a table nearby sat two empty cups and a plate of cookie crumbs.

Living Lemonade

Art always had a fondness for children despite the fact he had none of his own. Seldom had a child with something to sell knocked on Art's door and gone away without a sale, and the smaller the child the more Art seemed to buy.

One hot summer day, Art drove his car with the air-conditioner cranked up all the way as he headed to see his next client. Out of the corner of his eye he spotted a small boy selling lemonade.

Actually, two small boys headed up the enterprise. One frantically waved his arms to attract attention while the other remained seated behind a table selling lemonade. Art could not pass up an opportunity such as this.

"How much for a glass of lemonade?" Art asked as he pulled up and got out of his car.

"A small glass is a quarter and a large glass is fifty cents." The small boy beamed, happy to get a customer.

"Well, this is an awfully hot day," Art said. "I think I'll need a large glass."

"Yes, sir," the boy replied, grinning from ear to ear.

"What's your name, son?"

"Devan, sir. What's yours?"

"Art's the name. And that's Thirsty Art to you."

"Yes, sir, Thirsty Art," Devan replied, still grinning.

Art savored the lemonade and the moment.

"Had a lot of customers today, Devan?"

"Not really, you're only the third one. Second if you don't count my mom."

"Well, moms are awfully important, Devan. I think we need to count her."

Devan continued to grin.

"It's an awfully hot day, Devan. I think I'm going to need a second glass."

"Yes, sir," Devan replied, as he poured a refill and added another ice cube.

"This sure is the best lemonade I've ever had. Nothing like a good lemonade to quench a guy's thirst."

"Yes sir, but he who drinks my lemonade will thirst again, while he who drinks living lemonade will never thirst."

"You go to church, don't you, Devan?" Art asked as he thought back to the times when he and Patsy went to church before they divorced. Art did not want to quit going to church. He just felt like he did not fit in anymore.

"Every Sunday and Wednesday," Devan replied. "My dad's the pastor."

"Really!" Art answered. "Where's your church?"

Art and Devan continued to talk as Art sipped his lemonade. Art met Devan's mother, and Devan's dad drove in just before Art planned to leave.

Art did not get to see as many clients that day as he had planned, but he did promise to show up for church the following Sunday. As he drove off, he thought of the day when he would be able to tell about how he met the little lemonade-selling evangelist who turned his life around.

The Half-Empty Bed

Jill opened her still sleepy eyes and faced the empty part of the bed where Jack used to sleep. As was often the case, it was enough to jar Jill completely awake.

It had been six weeks since Jack left, but Jill still had trouble facing the fact that she might have to spend the rest of her life alone. Alone, and only thirty-two years of age.

As far as Jill could tell, Jack had not left her for another woman. That was one reason it had been so difficult for Jill to handle.

"Will memories of the good times be all I'll have left?" Jill asked herself as she thought back to all the kidding she and Jack took after they started dating.

"Remember, Jill, don't follow Jack up any hills," chirped one friend kiddingly.

And when they decided to get married another friend harped, "Are you sure you want to do this? You know what it means, don't you? Wherever Jack goes, you have to go tumbling after."

Jill wasn't even sure where Jack had gone. Oh she knew he had taken a small apartment while he sorted out his thoughts, but Jill had no idea what any of Jack's thoughts were. She had not heard from him, except when he stopped by to pick up Courtney. He always seemed uncomfortable whenever he stopped by for her.

The sad part was that Jill still loved Jack. She could not think of anything major that either of them had done wrong.

He always went to work, but never stayed late. He always had time for Courtney. He never drank and he was not abusive to her or Courtney.

"But we've drifted apart over the ten years we've been married," Jill thought to herself.

Jill looked at the clock. It had been over thirty minutes since she first awakened and began to think of Jack. Still, she did not yet feel like getting out of bed.

"But I must get out of bed. I have to try to put this out of my mind and think of Courtney. I know all of this has been so rough on her. A six year-old does not understand when her parents suddenly split up."

Jill's misery was interrupted by a knock at the door. She wiped her tears and called out, "Come in, Sweetheart."

Courtney opened the door and Jill was taken aback by the smile on Courtney's face.

"What are you so happy about?" her mother asked.

"Daddy's on the phone, and he wants to talk to *you*."

The words excited Jill, but she did not want to get her hopes up until she found out what Jack wanted. She slipped on her robe and hurried to the phone.

"Hi, Jack. Courtney said you had something you wanted to talk to me about."

"That's right, Jill, but I don't know where to begin."

"Just say what's on your mind, Jack. I'll listen."

"Okay, Jill. Jill, I've been thinking about us a lot ever since I left. I don't know how to explain it. I haven't been happy these last few months, but I still love you, and you know how much I love Courtney."

"Oh, Jack! I still love you, too!"

"Jill, I think I'd like for us to try to be a family again, but I don't want to go on the way we've been. I've felt an emptiness for quite some time. I can't go on that way. I don't think you know this, but three weeks ago I started going to church. It's a small church, so not only did I meet the pastor, but we've gotten to know each other a little bit. Jill, I'd like for you and Courtney to go to church with me this coming Sunday. While I don't think we're bad people, I think our main problem has been that we don't have a relationship with God. Now you don't have to answer me right now if you don't want to, you can think about...."

"Oh, Jack I don't need to think about it! Of course Courtney and I will go to church with you this Sunday! I've been thinking we needed to start going to church, but I was afraid you were against it, so I never mentioned it."

"That's been another one of our problems, Jill. We never took the time to talk about important things."

"Oh, I know that now, Jack."

"Is it okay if I stop by and pick you up a little after ten, or would you rather meet me at the church?"

"Of course you can stop by. You can even stop by or call before Sunday. Oh, Jack! I love you!"

"I love you, too, Jill! Oh, Jill! We have so much to talk about. I was thinking the three of us could go out to eat after church, and then it would be nice if we could figure out how you and I could get some time alone so we could talk."

"How about if you check with your mother to see if Courtney could spend the night with her?"

Eric & Annabelle

"Hello! Oh, I'm sorry. I didn't mean to startle you."

"You didn't startle me. I heard you coming a mile away."

"I was already here. You're the one who was coming."

"Whatever!"

"My name's Eric. What's yours?"

"Listen, will you be quiet? You'll scare the ducks away."

"Nothing will scare these guys away. Do you come here often?"

"Too often. Farnsworth makes me come every Friday."

"Farnsworth? Is he the man over by the car?"

"Yeah, Farnsworth's my driver."

"So why does Farnsworth make you come here every Friday if you don't want to come?"

"I don't know. He thinks it's good for me."

"It is good for you."

"And who are you? My shrink or something?"

"I already told you. I'm Eric, but I don't think you told me who you are."

"Well, if you must know, I'm Annabelle."

"Annabelle. What a pretty name for a pretty girl!"

"Well, I don't think it's a pretty name, and I wouldn't know a pretty girl if I saw one. I haven't seen too many of them lately."

"Well, I'd know a pretty girl if I saw one, and I'm seeing one now."

"Did Farnsworth pay you to say that to me?"

"Afraid not."

"Well, then why did you say it?"

"I believe in paying a compliment if it's genuine."

"Well, this time it's not genuine."

"Yes, it is."

"Let's just forget about talking about my looks."

"Okay, what would you like to talk about?"

"If I must be blunt to get my point across, nothing!"

"The ducks love people coming here to feed them, Annabelle. Just think of the joy you add to their lives."

"Listen, Mr. Pollyanna. Why do you insist on adding some joy to my life?"

"Because it's obvious there is none there already. Annabelle, how about you and I going somewhere together sometime?"

"Where would we go, dinner and a movie? In case you can't guess, Eric, I'm not much into movies these days."

"Me either. But dinner sounds good to me."

"Why, so you can watch me drop my food all over the place?"

"No, so I could put a little joy into both of our lives."

"Eric, in case you haven't noticed, I'm blind. There's no possibility of any joy entering my life."

"Blind? And here I thought you carried that cane in case someone asked you to do a Chaplin impersonation."

"Sorry, but you're not going to make me laugh."

"I think we found one thing on which we can agree. What do you do with the rest of your time, Annabelle? Stay home and feel sorry for yourself?"

"Well, Mr. Eric. If you were blind you might feel sorry for yourself, too. I think I've had enough of this conversation. Goodbye, Eric."

"Goodbye, Annabelle."

"Are you ready to go Miss?"

"Boy, am I ready to go, Farnsworth!"

"Miss Annabelle, who was that gentleman in the wheelchair you were talking to?"

"Wh...wh...wheelchair?"

"Yes, Miss. Didn't he tell you?"

"No, Farnsworth, he didn't. Farnsworth, is he still there?"

"Yes, Miss. He's sitting there enjoying the ducks."

"Farnsworth, are we in a big hurry today?"

19

"I don't know about we, Miss, but I'm not in a hurry, but then I'm never the one who's in a hurry to leave."

"Farnsworth, the gentleman's name is Eric and I believe I'll go back and visit with him some more. Mind watching my cane for a few minutes?"

"But what if you fall, Miss?"

"I'll get back up, of course! What did you think I'd do?"

Entertaining Angels

"May I help you, sir?" the receptionist asked.

"Yes, I'd like to see Mr. Angell."

"I'm sorry, sir, but there's no one here by that name."

"But there must be. I just talked with him last Thursday."

"Maybe you have our business confused with another business."

"No, I was here last Thursday. I had a job interview with Mr. Stan Angell right there in that office."

"But that's Mr. Hardison's office, sir."

"I don't know whose office it is, but the man who interviewed me told me his name was Stan Angell. Listen, I'm not here to make trouble. I just want to thank Mr. Angell."

"I don't know what to tell you, sir. Will you excuse me a moment while I check with Mr. Hardison and see if he can help you?"

"Of course," the man replied as the receptionist turned away.

The receptionist walked over and knocked on the office door. She returned a couple of minutes later.

"Mr. Hardison says he will speak with you now. You may go in."

"Come in, sir. Now, how may I help you?"

"I'm sorry to bother you. I came looking for Mr. Angell, but the receptionist doesn't seem to know him."

"That's because we have no Mr. Angell."

"But there's his picture hanging behind your desk."

"But that's my father!"

"I don't know who he is, but last Thursday he told me he was Mr. Angell."

"You saw my father last Thursday?"

"That's right. Right in this office."

"And why were you here last Thursday?"

21

"I saw an ad in the paper about a job opening. You did have an ad in the paper about a job opening, didn't you?"

"Yes, but I'm sorry to say that it's already been filled."

"That's okay. I have a job thanks to Mr. Angell, your father, or whomever the gentlemen was."

"Maybe you'd like to explain to me, Mr...."

"Thompson. Alan Thompson."

"Maybe you'd like to explain to me, Mr. Thompson."

"I'd be happy to. Three months ago I lost my job. I'd been trying to find a new one ever since. I didn't have any luck. My wife was getting discouraged. Just the night before I talked to Mr. Angell I got down on my knees and prayed and asked God to help me get a job. Then I saw your ad in the newspaper. I called and talked to Mr. Angell. He told me he would be happy to interview me last Thursday at noon."

"At noon, you say?"

"That's right, noon."

"I don't suppose you know that the office is always locked from 12:00-1:00 while everyone goes to lunch."

"Well, come to think of it, no one else was here except Mr. Angell and me."

"Go on, Mr. Thompson."

"Well, Mr. Angell and I talked for a few minutes. He was such a pleasant old man. Oh, sorry, I didn't mean anything bad about that. Anyway, Mr. Angell told me he thought I was over-qualified for the position, but he recommended another company who was going to be needing someone. He called them, got me an interview, and I got the job. Funny thing was that they were just about to advertise the job when Mr. Angell called them. Not only did they hire me, but they gave me more money than I made at my other job. I just came back to thank Mr. Angell for helping me get the job. Funny thing about that old man, I mean your father."

"What's that, Mr. Thompson?"

"Well, the way he kept pulling out that red handkerchief with the white polka dots and wiping his brow, you'd think he was the one who needed the job. Mr. Hardison, did I say something wrong? Are you okay?"

"I'm...I'm fine, I guess. You say the man had a red handkerchief with white polka dots?"

"That's right. You know him then? Was it your father?"

"Well, yes and no."

"What do you mean by 'yes and no?'"

"Well, my father had a handkerchief just like that, and he was always taking it out and wiping his brow."

"Then it must have been your father who interviewed me. But why did he use the name Mr. Angell?"

"Mr. Thompson, I don't know how to tell you this. My father has been dead for twenty years."

Bob's Christmas

When most people make plans to get married, they expect their marriage to last a long time. Bob did not. Bob knew his marriage would be short-lived, but he decided to get married anyway. It was not that Bob lacked commitment. It was that Kathy lacked time. The doctors told Kathy that she would not live until Christmas. She almost made it, but on December 18th she left the hospital and moved on to heaven.

Bob and Kathy met in the hospital. Both of them were patients. Bob got better, but Kathy did not. It did not take Bob long to fall in love with Kathy, but then everyone loved Kathy because she was easy to love. Their romance lasted a several month stay for both of them. Then, two months after Bob was discharged, Bob and Kathy married.

Kathy told Bob that marrying her was useless, but nothing she said could change his mind. Bob loved Kathy. He loved her very much and getting married was his way of showing it. Bob kidded Kathy that her wedding gown was like no wedding gown he had seen, and he especially liked the opening in the back, but then Bob and Kathy were always kidding one another.

Neither Bob nor Kathy had any family. Still, several men and women came to the wedding, because many people loved Bob and Kathy. Wedding guests consisted of discharged patients, patients able to get out of bed, off-duty doctors and nurses, and other patients' families. People crowded closely to the hospital bed. Kathy was too weak to get out of bed to be married.

After they married, Bob continued to come to the hospital every day and sit and hold Kathy's hand as they talked and prayed together. Bob arrived early every morning before work, came again at noon, and returned each evening until the lights were turned out for the night. Bob stopped by for a few minutes on Sunday before heading off to church, and he came back shortly after the service to share with Kathy all that the pastor had said.

The days that followed Kathy's death were difficult for Bob, because he had nowhere to go. Oh, he went to the cemetery each day, but he still had a lot of long lonely hours at home.

Christmas Eve was a particularly tough time for Bob. For most people Christmas Eve was a happy time. For Bob it was a lonely time. On the Christmas Eve after Kathy died, Bob picked up his Bible and began to read the Christmas story from Luke. He read it and then read it again. As he finished the second time, he put down his Bible and began to pray.

While in the midst of prayer, the doorbell rang. Bob had no idea who it was. He was not expecting anyone. Bob rose from his chair and headed off to satisfy his curiosity.

At the door he found Larry and Norma Baker, Ken's parents. Ken had also been a hospital patient, and Ken died just a couple of weeks before Kathy.

"Why, Larry and Norma! This is a surprise! Please come in! What brings you out on Christmas Eve?"

"We got up lonely this morning, so we tried to think who would know what we were feeling. We thought of you and immediately decided to go shopping. These are for you," Norma said as she handed him an armload of presents.

Bob laid down the presents and hugged Larry and Norma. Everyone's tears flowed freely.

"Tissue, anyone?" Bob asked, as they separated and he picked up a box of facial tissues.

"Why, Bob? Don't you remember? I 'tished' you when we came in the door," Norma replied.

Laughter replaced their solemn moment.

"Just for that, Norma, I'm going to make some hot chocolate and open the tin of cookies I bought today."

"Punishment like that I can handle anytime," Norma kidded.

"Have a seat. I'll be back as soon as the hot chocolate's ready," Bob said as he turned to leave the room.

Larry and Norma sat down and looked around the room familiarizing themselves with Bob's house.

"Well, here we are, and there's more if you want it," Bob said as he carried in a tray.

Joy replaced the emptiness that had engulfed these three people's hearts just a short time before.

"You two have made this evening special for me," Bob said. "Now, I'd like to do what I can to return the favor."

With that Bob picked up his Bible and began to read the Christmas story, only this time he had someone to share it with.

The Good Neighbor Game

The howling wind awakened Mrs. Potter. She felt toasty underneath her many quilts, but she had to know if the weatherman's forecast was right. She flipped back the covers and eased her feet over the side of the bed.

She moved slowly through her darkened bedroom, inched over to the window, pulled open the drapes, and cracked the blind. As she peered through the slit she had mixed emotions.

The snow that blanketed her front yard sparkled like diamonds. The full moon created dancing shadows as the trees moved back and forth in the wind.

Still, all that snow meant work for her in the morning. Work she did not look forward to doing. Of course, she would only have to shovel the snow if her neighbor, Ben Rynierson, did not beat her to it.

Mrs. Potter smiled as she thought of the kindly gentleman who lived next-door. She lingered for a moment as she enjoyed the beautiful scene before her.

Suddenly a chill came over her. She quickly remembered how warm she had been under all those quilts. She closed the drapes, scurried back to bed, and drifted off to sleep.

Several hours later Mrs. Potter was awakened by the sound of a snow shovel.

"It's Ben Rynierson again, I'm sure," she thought to herself.

Once again, only with plenty of daylight this time, Mrs. Potter flipped back the covers and headed to the window.

Sure enough, Mr. Rynierson, at seventy-six years old, four years her senior, had almost finished clearing her sidewalk.

As she spied on her next-door neighbor, she was interrupted by the ringing of the telephone.

"Hello. Oh, hi, Molly. No, you don't need to send Jack over to shovel my walk. You know who did it again.

"Oh, Molly, quit your kidding. Benjamin Rynierson isn't interested in me. He's just a good neighbor. That's all! I just wish he'd shovel his own walk first. But I'm going to fix him this time.

"Oh, it's not how I'm going to fix him. It's what I'm going to fix him. I'm going to fix him a big pot of soup. You know Callie always did all the cooking, and I'm not sure he always eats well now that she's gone. Well, he'll eat well for the next couple of days.

"No, you don't have to go to the store for me. I've got everything I need right here.

"Sure, you can stop by later. Just don't go to any trouble. Well, goodbye. See you this afternoon sometime."

Mrs. Potter hung up the phone eager to show Mr. Rynierson that two could play this "good neighbor" game.

Some time later, armed with a kettle of soup and its pleasant aroma, Mrs. Potter donned her hat, coat, scarf, and a smile, as she headed off on her mission.

Mr. Rynierson had done such a good job of shoveling her sidewalk that she did not slide as she made her way to the house next door.

"Why, Katherine Potter! What brings you out on a day like this?" Mr. Rynierson asked as he opened his front door.

"You do, Ben Rynierson."

"Well, whatever for?"

"Let's just say that I looked out my window this morning and I saw someone shoveling my walk, and he was wearing your coat."

"You don't say! Well, I've always been willing to loan my coat if someone had a need for it."

"I'm sure you would. And wasn't it convenient that the man was just your size?"

"I guess it helps to be normal size, Katherine. So many people don't keep in shape these days."

"Shoveling snow always keeps a person in shape if they don't overdo it. Of course, I never get a chance to find out, because someone always shovels my walk before I get a chance. You know how that is, don't you, Ben?"

"Of course, but those things happen sometimes, Katherine."

"They do, Benjamin, but then it leaves me with so much time on my hands that I have to do something. This morning I decided to make some soup. It's hard to make soup for one person, and I didn't want the rest of the soup to go to waste."

"Smells mighty good, Katherine."

"The vegetables are as fresh as I could get this time of year. By the way, Ben, do you need anything from the store? Molly's coming over later."

"You sure it wouldn't be any trouble?"

"Not at all. You know Molly. She'd be delighted."

"Well, I didn't know I'd be eating soup today, and I like crackers with my soup. Do you think she could pick up a box for me?"

"I don't know. You know how heavy a box of crackers is. But I imagine she'll be able to manage somehow," Mrs. Potter replied as she smiled.

That night it snowed again, though not as much as the night before. The next morning Mr. Rynierson awakened to the sound of someone shoveling snow.

He looked out the window and saw that Mrs. Potter had almost finished shoveling his walk. He hastily went to the phone to call another neighbor to find out how someone would go about making homemade soup.

First Date

Doug and Cindy sat nervously on the living room couch. Every few minutes Cindy looked at her watch.

"What time is it?" Doug asked.

"Five minutes later than the last time you asked," Cindy answered.

"And what time is that?"

"It's 8:30, Doug!"

"And what time did we tell her to be home?" Doug asked.

"Ten o'clock."

"Ten o'clock! That's kind of late, isn't it?"

"I don't know, Doug. Rachel thought it was kind of early."

"Early! I didn't get to stay out that late until I was sixteen."

"Doug, Rachel *is* sixteen."

"Yeah, but she's a girl! When I was sixteen I was a boy."

"I would hope so, Doug."

"Yeah, but isn't ten o'clock kind of late?"

"Are we back to this again?"

"Sorry, hon. What time is it now?"

"It's 8:32! That means it's two minutes later than the last time you asked. Your asking is getting closer each time."

"Kind of like contractions, huh, Cindy?"

"I'll pretend I didn't hear that one."

"Did you check out this boy before you let her go out with him?"

"Doug, are you there?"

"Am I where, Cindy?"

"Are you anywhere? Remember, Rachel went out with Tommy."

"Tommy who?"

"Tommy Oliver. You know. The boy that lives next door."

"I thought he looked familiar."

"Doug, sometimes you're impossible."

"It's called being a dad. You know, Cindy. I think we should've gone with them."

"I don't think they would've gone for that."

"Well, maybe we should've followed them. Do you have any idea where they were going?"

"Yes, Doug! And you would too, if you'd paid any attention when I told you they were going out."

"Fill me in again, hon."

"It was a party at church."

"What church, Cindy? It isn't one of those cults, is it?"

"Doug! Hello! Remember, the Olivers go to the same church we do."

"Oh, that Tommy who lives next door."

"Yes, Doug."

"What was that? Did you hear something, Cindy?"

"Yes, Doug. It was your mouth again."

"No, it sounded like a car."

"No, Doug. A car is much quieter than your mouth."

"I resent that, Cindy. I guess I'm just more of a concerned parent than you are."

"Doug, I probably shouldn't tell you this, but I'm just as nervous as you are."

"Whew! And I thought I was the only one who was worried."

"Cindy."

"What now, Doug?"

"Do you think he'll kiss her?"

"Not if you're waiting by the curb when they get home."

"You mean it's okay if I wait outside?"

"No, Doug. I was just kidding."

"How about if I just stand in the front door with the porch light on?"

"How about if you go to the grocery?"

"You need something, Cindy?"

"Yes, Doug. I could use a little peace and quiet."

"What department is that in?"

31

"I don't know, but if I ever find out I'll be sure and get some."

Ten o'clock could not come quickly enough for Cindy. Finally, it came.

"I know I heard something that time, Cindy."

"Doug, sit down! I'll look out the window."

"Is it them, Cindy?"

"Yes, Doug. It's them."

"How close is she sitting to him, Cindy?"

"I don't know, Doug. I can only make out one person. Sit down, Doug! I was just kidding."

"He's not ...you know, is he?"

"No, I don't know, Doug."

"You know, Cindy. Kissing our baby."

"You mean that thing we used to do, Doug?"

"What do you mean 'used to,' Cindy?"

"Well, I meant back when you could really kiss."

"You mean you don't think I'm a good kisser anymore?"

"I'm kidding, Doug. Well, would you look at that?"

"Look at what, Cindy?"

"Doug, sit down! I'm just kidding."

"How about if I look out the window and do the kidding for a change?"

"Doug, sit down! Quick! He's walking her to the door!"

"Good night, Tommy. I had a good time," Rachel said as she opened the door.

"Oh, hi, Mom and Dad. What are you two still doing up?"

"Oh, it's still early yet," Doug answered.

"But Dad, you're always in bed before ten."

"Oh, is it ten already? My how time flies. I didn't realize it was that late. Did you, Cindy?"

"Uh, no."

"Okay, Mom and Dad. Whatever you say. By the way, Mom. You need to fix the blind. That one is stuck at just about your eye level. And just in case you couldn't see well enough, he didn't kiss me goodbye, he gave me big hug instead."

"Cindy."

"What is it, Doug?"

"Which is worse, hon? A kiss or a big hug?" Doug asked Cindy, as Rachel wondered how in the world she would be able to raise her parents over the next few years.

The Compassionate Stranger

The stranger entered the large church and took a seat near the front. At first, people only noticed that his clothes did not measure up to those of the rest of the congregation, but then everyone realized that the stranger had sat in Mrs. Jenkins' pew.

No one sat in Mrs. Jenkins's pew. No one except Mrs. Jenkins, of course. No one else dared. Neighbors whispered to one another. Each wondered what Mrs. Jenkins would do when she made her grand entrance.

They did not have long to wait. Mrs. Jenkins arrived at the back of the church and began her trek down the aisle without a clue as to what awaited her. As she neared the front of the church she began to count as she always did. "One, two, three, four, five, six, seven, eight." When she got to eight she saw someone sitting there, so she began to count again only to come to the same conclusion.

Mrs. Jenkins inched forward so that the stranger could see her. She hoped he would understand and beat a hasty retreat. The stranger looked at her and smiled, but Mrs. Jenkins did not return his smile.

When it was obvious the stranger had found his resting place, at least as far as that service was concerned, Mrs. Jenkins let out an indignant "excuse me" and pushed past him into the pew.

During the service, the stranger could not help but notice Mrs. Jenkins was more concerned with him occupying part of her pew than she was in getting anything from or contributing anything to the service.

They came to a point in the service where the pastor invited everyone to come to the altar to pray. The stranger rose and went forward. There was no need for him to hurry because this did not seem to be a part of anyone else's exercise program that morning.

The stranger fell to his knees and began in earnest prayer. He prayed for quite some time until someone tapped him on the shoulder. Standing above him was a man who looked just as "welcoming" as Mrs. Jenkins. Could he be a relative of hers?

"Excuse me, but could you return to your seat so the pastor can get on with the sermon?" the man asked in an indignant manner.

The stranger rose and returned to his seat. As he returned to row eight he noticed that Mrs. Jenkins had scooted over to occupy the aisle seat he once occupied. This time she smiled a triumphant smile.

Mrs. Jenkins sat forward in the pew. She hoped that her actions would cause the stranger to choose a different pew, but her hopes were soon dashed. He said "excuse me" as he moved past her into the pew. As the stranger sat down and turned to return Mrs. Jenkins' smile, he found her smile had already gotten tired and had fallen into a frown.

The service continued and concluded at the expected hour. The pastor knew he had to finish on time, unless he wanted to preach to an empty church.

Before Mrs. Jenkins could leave, the stranger turned to her and reached out his hand to shake hers. Taken by surprise, the stranger managed to clasp Mrs. Jenkins's hand before she could pull it away.

As his nail-scarred hand took hers, it was as if scales fell from Mrs. Jenkins's eyes. For the first time she realized who the stranger was. Her tears flowed down her cheeks. The stranger embraced Mrs. Jenkins as they began to talk and after a few moments the two of them headed to the altar to pray. No one had noticed, because there was no one left to notice.

The following Sunday people were immersed in typical pre-service conversation. A hush fell over the crowd as Mrs. Jenkins arrived. Not only was she accompanied by the stranger from the week before, but she had stopped by the orphanage and picked up a carload of boys whom she instructed into the pew ahead of her. Mrs. Jenkins's face glowed. She looked twenty years younger.

After Mrs. Jenkins and all the boys were seated, the stranger excused himself, turned away, and went to take a seat next to the man who had tapped him on the shoulder the week before. The puffed-up man had no idea he was about to make a new-found friend.

A Gift From God

Jack and Karen liked remembering, but they liked forgetting just as much. They liked remembering all the wonderful things Becca did, while they tried to forget the day a passing motorist took away her life. While each of them smiled on occasion, too often they felt nothing but numbness, sadness, and grief.

Someone told Jack and Karen that a change of scenery might help. One day they sold their home and left. They hoped to begin a new life. They built a home that looked nothing like the old one, a home they built in the middle of nowhere where motorists passed like the seasons, one every three months.

God made this possible when He blessed Jack with a talent for writing. As a part-time author with a full-time career, Jack submitted a book which a publisher liked. Soon, he followed it up with a second book. A third book contained characters with whom enough people identified that it launched a successful series of books and provided the funds for a change of career and scenery.

Karen hoped that the change in scenery would remove all her pain. It did help, but nothing would ever repair the hole in her heart.

Jack tried his best to help. He was there for Karen whenever he sensed her sinking. They turned to Scripture and prayer for answers, and while they did not get all their questions answered, they did find comfort.

"If only I can get pregnant again," Karen thought, but God never answered that prayer. Still, Karen prayed faithfully every day.

When Karen got up one morning, she had no idea that God would answer her prayer in a way she had never thought possible.

As the sausage sizzled in the skillet, Karen thought she heard someone knocking at the door.

"My ears must be playing tricks on me. Jack's inside. We haven't had a visitor since we moved here, and besides, if there's any sound I would recognize, it would be the sound of a car or truck," Karen thought to herself.

Karen dismissed the thought and went back to fixing breakfast, only this time the knock was loud enough there was no mistaking the fact that someone stood outside their front door.

"Jack! Can you get the door? I'm busy fixing breakfast."

"Are you sure someone's at the door?" Jack called back.

"Yeah, they've knocked twice now," Karen replied.

"Wonder who it could be? Anyway, you'll have to get it because I just got out of the shower and I'm not dressed yet."

Karen laid down her spatula, walked across the hardwood floor and peered through the curtain. She saw no one.

"It must have been the wind," she thought.

Just as Karen turned away, she heard the knock again. She got to the door just as Jack ambled down the stairs.

"Who is it, hon?" Jack asked, but Karen, overcome with emotion, could not answer.

Jack walked to the door. Tears streamed down Karen's cheeks. Jack looked down at what Karen had already seen, a baby lying in a basket.

Jack and Karen had heard stories such as this. They had even read about it in books and had seen it in movies.

Jack darted past Karen out the door to see who had brought the baby.

When he returned, Karen said, "You didn't see anyone, did you?"

"Not even a tire track or a footprint, and I even went around back."

Karen reached down to lift the baby out of the basket and found a note.

"My name is Ashley," the note said. "I'm your new daughter. If you check with the adoption agency you will find all the papers have been filled out."

As Karen held the baby in her left arm, she gasped and covered her mouth with her right hand. Karen looked for a tissue to dry her tears.

Jack called the sheriff to find out who might have left this precious little girl on their doorstep.

"May I have your address, please?" the sheriff asked.

"6324 Dry Creek Road," Jack answered.

"Oh, you must be Mr. Ambrose," the sheriff replied.

"That's right! How did you know?"

"Oh, I knew a family built a house out there. Believe it or not, I was just about to call you and let you know that last night's storm knocked over several trees and flooded Ford's Creek, so there's no way you can get out of there until the clean-up crew is finished and the water level goes down. I just wanted to know if you're okay and if you have everything you need for your baby?"

"Who says we have a baby?" Jack asked.

"Well, it says right here, Jack and Karen Ambrose and their daughter Ashley. According to the birth date Ashley is six weeks old today. You must be very happy!"

"Yes, very happy," Jack managed to whisper as he turned and hung up the phone.

Kristen's Sacrifice

Kristen bounded down the stairs. She failed to show any resemblance to the graceful descent she expected to display the following week when she planned to head off to the senior prom with Jay. Kristen looked forward to the prom more than any other event during her final year of high school.

Kristen thought back to the times she had sat on the floor at her mother's feet. She had her mother tell her all about her own prom -- the dress, the corsage and where they went for dinner. Kristen had them all memorized, but she loved to hear her mother recall the memories of her senior year. Hearing her mother's memories seemed to strengthen their relationship, and looking ahead to her prom the following week made Kristen feel grown up.

Only the Saturday before, Kristen and her mom had gone shopping for the right prom dress. She tried on nine dresses before she made her selection, a strapless emerald green gown to go with her auburn hair.

"What's the matter, Kristen?" her mom asked as she turned in the car to see her daughter's glowing smile turn into tears.

"I'm just so happy, Mom. I know you and Dad aren't rich. I still have the dress I wore to the junior prom in my closet, and yet you and Dad were willing to buy me a new dress."

"That old thing. Hey, girl, you only get to be a senior once, and your Dad and I know how much having a new dress for the prom means to you."

"Am I spoiled, Mom?"

"Probably, but a good spoiled."

"Well, I just want you and Dad to know how grateful I am," Kristen said as she unbuckled her seat beat and slid over to give her mom a hug.

"Hey, buckle up! I'm not going to take off until you do. Besides we have to hurry home so we can show off your dress to your dad and Tommy."

"Why Tommy? What do little brothers know? Remember last year, 'Look, tomboy has a dress on.'"

"Well, it might have been the first time Tommy saw you in a dress."

"No, it wasn't. Remember I wore one to granddaddy's funeral."

"Okay, the second time."

"Besides, Jay doesn't mind that I wear jeans all the time."

"You've got a point there, girl. If Jay and your dad approve, who cares what Tommy thinks?"

Kristen rounded the corner to the living room and saw her mom talking on the phone. She looked as if she had heard some bad news. Kristen's focus quickly changed from the weekend before when she and her mom picked out a prom dress together to wondering what had upset her mom.

As soon as her mother hung up the phone, Kristen pumped her.

"What's wrong, Mom? Is everybody okay?"

"It's the Thompson's, dear. They had a fire. No one was hurt, but they lost everything."

"Everything?"

"I'm afraid so."

"What are they going to do?"

"I don't know. They're staying with Mrs. Thompson's parents over on Claymoore Avenue for a few days until they get everything sorted out."

"How's Keri doing?"

"I'd say she's happy to be alive, but she's devastated from the loss."

"We were planning to double for the prom, Keri and Jason, and Jay and I. Now, I wonder if she'll even go. I sure hope she does. I think it would be good for her."

"Me, too," her mom agreed. "Everyone needs a positive diversion at a time like this. I sure hope she still goes, too."

"Mom, if you don't mind I'm going to my room. I've got some thinking to do."

"That's fine, dear. Remember I'm here if you need to talk."

"You and Dad are always here for us, Mom, and I'm forever grateful."

"As grateful as you were to get the dress?" her mom asked.

"More."

With that Kristen turned and headed up the stairs, not in her normal three steps at a time gate, but slowly, using the banister to pull herself up.

After several minutes of lying across the bed in deep thought, Kristen once again emerged from her room and bounded down the stairs.

"Mom!"

"In here, dear."

"Mom, I've got a question."

"Shoot."

"Well, Mom, I've been thinking. You know, about Keri and the Thompsons."

"Yes, dear?"

"I hope you're not upset. I don't think you will be."

"Upset about the Thompsons?"

"You know I don't mean upset about the Thompsons. I mean upset about what I want to do."

"I'm never upset about anything you want to do. You know that."

"I know. Well, I've been thinking. Since Keri lost everything in that fire, what would you think if I gave her some of my clothes? I've really got more than I need."

"I think that would be great! Carolyn said the Thompson's could use practically anything."

"I wasn't thinking of practically anything. I was even thinking of giving her my prom dress if she's still going."

"That's sweet of you, dear. I doubt if anyone would recognize it as the dress you wore last year."

"You know what I mean, Mom. I'll be the one wearing the one I wore last year. I plan to give Keri my new one."

"Why I think that's wonderful! Whatever possessed you to think of something like that?"

"I'm not sure. It could be heredity and it could be environment."

Christmas Morning

Most Christmas mornings Emma Rose sprang from her bed like a four-year-old. One Christmas she yanked the covers over her head and hoped the day went away.

Scrooge had not brainwashed her. Emma Rose did not detest Christmas all of a sudden. She hated her new set of circumstances. Not only were there no presents under the tree, there was no tree. It was Emma Rose's first year without; without a tree, without presents, without Milburn.

Only a few months before, Emma Rose and Milburn celebrated their forty-ninth wedding anniversary. They looked forward to celebrating number fifty. But then Emma Rose and Milburn enjoyed celebrating everything.

Both of them enjoyed life and lived it to the fullest. Before they could celebrate their golden wedding anniversary, Milburn's heart gave out.

Most of her life, Emma Rose rose each morning before daylight. But the loneliness that accompanied Milburn's death had robbed her of all the joy and excitement she had for the upcoming days, weeks, and months. Emptiness had moved in and kicked all of the joy out of Emma Rose's heart.

But just as she had done every day since Milburn's death, Emma Rose realized that she would have to face Christmas morning no matter what it held.

One at a time Emma Rose eased her feet over the side of her bed until both of them touched the hardwood floor. For forty-nine years, each Christmas morning, Emma Rose tiptoed to the kitchen and started breakfast, so that Milburn awakened to the smell of bacon, eggs, homemade biscuits, and hot coffee.

But without Milburn, Emma Rose had to force herself to make a cup of coffee and a bowl of hot oatmeal, with a little cinnamon and brown sugar mixed in. Just as she finished washing the bowl, cup, and saucer, the doorbell rang.

"Who could that be?" she wondered.

Emma Rose's slippers slid across the hardwood floor to the front door. When she got there, she cracked open the door. A blast of cold air entered.

Emma Rose peered through the crack in the door. Her tears began to flow, as she saw a "who's who of the neighborhood" perched on her front porch.

"We have some things for you, Miss Emma Rose," Molly Hatcher said.

"Well, I'll declare! Come on in, everyone."

Twenty-three people stepped inside the house. Each person carried something. Joe and Ed carried in the Christmas tree. Others toted sacks containing ornaments and lights. Still others had presents to go under the tree after it was decorated. Molly and Miss Paula had a Christmas ham and all the fixings.

"Do you want to help decorate the tree, Miss Emma Rose, or do you just want to watch?" Sadie Tackett, the street's second oldest citizen asked.

"Why don't I just sit here and watch you do it."

"As you wish, Miss Emma. As you wish."

While some took the food to the kitchen, others pitched in and decorated the tree. Once the tree was decorated, an assembly line formed to pass the presents to those closest to the tree.

"I hope you like what we got you, Miss Emma Rose," Billy Hatcher said excitedly.

"Oh, I'm sure I will, Billy. I'm sure I will. Just having friends like all of you is enjoyment enough."

"Do you want to open them now, Miss Emma Rose?" asked Billy's little brother Jason.

"Whatever you want me to do, Jason. What do you think?"

"I think you should go ahead."

"Then go ahead it is. Which one do you want me to open first?"

"How about this shiny red one? It's from us. I helped mom pick it out."

Emma Rose spent the next forty-five minutes crying all over the presents as she opened them. She was exhausted from the ordeal, but much happier than when she awoke.

After a few more minutes of sharing the love Jesus taught them to share and after the food was put away until dinner, Emma Rose handed out hugs to twenty-three people, some of whom got more than one. And then it came time for everyone to leave.

"We saved the best present for last, Miss Emma Rose, but we thought you might want to wait until we'd left before you open it."

Molly Hatcher reached into her pocket and handed Emma Rose an envelope. After everyone left, Emma Rose sat down in her favorite rocker and opened the envelope and began to read its contents.

"My most precious Emma Rose," it began. "Recently, I felt the Lord telling me that I might not have much time left. I want to write some words to leave for you. After I write this letter, I'll give it to Molly Hatcher and ask her if she'll give this to you the first Christmas you're all alone. I just want to let you know that while I may not be around any more, I'm up in heaven loving you just as much."

"I hope you haven't lost your excitement for Christmas, just because I'm not there to celebrate it with you. Remember how we used to...."

Divide And Multiply

Mary struggled to get by each winter. Her bills went up while her income went down.

One wintry day Mary's refrigerator sat empty. Her only food consisted of peanut butter, bread, and bananas. Mary had only enough for two sandwiches and there were four more days until she got paid again, but Mary never worried. She knew God wrapped His everlasting arms around her every day, summer or winter.

As Mary prepared to sit down and eat half of her bounty, she heard a knock at the door.

"May I help you?" Mary asked as she opened the door to see a stranger standing and shivering before her.

"Could you spare a crust of bread?" the stranger asked.

"No," Mary said, "but I could make you a peanut butter and banana sandwich."

"That sounds wonderful," the stranger answered. "Mind if I wait here on the porch?"

"Yes, I do mind," Mary replied. "But you could come in and eat it at the table."

Not expecting both food and warmth, the stranger eagerly entered the house.

"Would you like to warm yourself by the fire while I fix the sandwiches?"

"That would be nice, if you don't mind."

Mary left the stranger and hurried off to the kitchen to the last four pieces of bread, the last two bananas, and the bottom of the jar of peanut butter.

In a few minutes she returned.

"Supper is ready. I'm sorry, but I only have hot tea and water to drink. Which would you like?"

"If you have enough hot tea, that sounds great."

"Hot tea, it is," Mary replied.

Mary made and poured the tea and she and the stranger sat down to eat.

"Lord, I thank you for your bounty. In Jesus name. Amen."

"Amen," repeated the stranger.

"Where are you from?" Mary asked.

"Oh, no place in particular."

"Where are you staying now?"

"Well, I don't really have a place right now."

"Well, where do you plan to stay tonight?"

"I haven't really thought about it."

"I assume that means you don't have anywhere to stay."

"Well, not yet, anyway."

"Well, now you do, if the couch is good enough for you."

"Good enough! It would be more than good enough!"

"Well, I'll bring you some blankets after we eat. I bet you're tired and would like to get to sleep."

"Well, yeah, I really am tired, and it sure would be nice to get to sleep without the biting wind whipping in my face."

After they finished eating, Mary headed to the linen closet. She located a sheet, a couple of blankets, a towel, and a wash cloth and handed them to the stranger.

"The bathroom is in there in case you want to wash up."

"That would be nice."

Mary left the stranger and headed off to her room.

Upon awakening the next morning, Mary remembered the stranger.

"How will I tell him I have nothing for breakfast?" she asked herself.

Mary dressed and then opened the door slightly. "Are you awake?"

There was no answer, so Mary called out again. "Are you awake, sir?"

Again she received no answer. Mary headed to the living room where she found the sheet and blankets neatly folded and an envelope lying on top of them.

Mary opened the envelope and found a note which read, "Because you were willing to give, you have received."

Mary had no idea what the stranger meant until she went into the kitchen and found her refrigerator and cabinets stocked with food.

A Greater Hope

Many who knew Ray only by reputation, but knew nothing of his situation, were eager to trade places with him. Many knew Ray simply as the most successful Christian romance novelist in the business. They knew nothing of his condition. That was the way Ray wanted it.

At thirty-seven years of age, Ray was twenty years removed from the house fire that took the lives of the rest of his family. In one cruel night Ray lost his parents, a brother, and three sisters. Ray was the only survivor -- if that was what you wanted to call him.

Ray suffered from constant pain which increased each time he typed on the keyboard. Ray had been told that there were computers available which would allow him to write without touching the keys. To Ray the pain of writing reminded him of the pain that remained in his heart.

The general public thought no one could write about love as well as Ray. With each new book his words warmed the hearts of many a female, both young and old alike. Only God knew how many girls and women had put themselves into the pages of one of Ray's books and had shed a few tears on the pages of those books.

It had been years since Ray had gone out in public. The innocent comments of small children and the stares of adults took their toll on an already hurting young man.

Ray moved away to a place where no one knew him and the only people he saw were his doctor and nurse who called on him regularly to treat him. Even the grocery boy left the order on the stoop outside the back door.

Ray had only one friend. Ray and Katherine stayed in touch each day by e-mail. Since he did not use his real name, Katherine had no idea that Ray was a successful novelist, nor did she know anything from his past. Instead, they wrote back and forth and had developed a friendship which made Ray think what might have been.

Ray suffered from constant pain, both emotionally and physically. Still, he took time every day to praise God for allowing him to touch the lives of so many people. Ray would never know true happiness, but that did not keep him from blessing others through his writing.

While Ray would never know what happiness was, he experienced joy. Ray's joy was that he served a risen Savior who had given him a gift and a talent that allowed him to touch the lives of others.

God had spoken to Ray and had let him know that among his readers were those who would know love only through the words he wrote. That was enough to keep Ray going back each day to endure the pain of another day's assignment.

While Ray was not blessed with the everyday blessings others took for granted, his life was filled with hope that many others did not have. For Ray looked forward to that day when he would no longer suffer. Ray looked forward to that day when he would see his parents and his brothers and sisters once again. Ray looked forward to that day when he would meet his one true Friend face-to-face. Ray knew he could not have a greater hope than that.

Embarrassing Or Embracing?

"What's wrong, Nicole?"

"Nothing, Mom."

"Nicole, this is your mother. Remember? What's wrong?"

"Aw, Mom. You know."

"It's the braces, isn't it?"

"Yeah. Why does school have to start this soon?"

"It's bound to start sooner or later. You might as well get it over with."

"Yeah, and over and over and over. That's what I'm afraid of."

"It won't be that bad. You'll get to see Eric."

"That's what I'm afraid of. Remember how I started to like him at the end of the year. What if he doesn't like my braces?"

"I guess you'll just have to talk to God about it, Nicole."

"But, Mom. Does God really care about my braces?"

"God cares about all of you. Why don't you ask him to help you get through tomorrow?"

"Okay, if you think it'll help. But if not, I'm going to change schools on Tuesday."

"Well, I don't think it'll come to that. You'll be okay. Trust me, and most of all, trust God to help you deal with it."

"Okay, Mom. I'll try."

"You want me to stay and pray with you."

"No, that's okay. God and I can handle it by ourselves."

"Okay, I'll cut out the light."

Nicole's prayers helped her through the night, but it took all the courage she could muster to head to school the next day. She almost made it through the day without running into Eric, only to find him seated next to her in her last class.

Nicole had kept her lips pressed together all day. Somehow, she even managed to get through lunch without anyone noticing, but then no one had told a joke that day until Nicole got to Mr. Bradley's class.

Mr. Bradley delivered one of his notoriously funny jokes and caught Nicole unprepared. Not only did she grin, but without thinking she turned to face a grinning Eric.

Nicole and Eric's eyes got big as neither could believe what they saw.

"You've got braces, too!" they echoed.

"Cool!" Eric said.

"Yeah, cool!" Nicole replied.

"Hey, Nicole. Can I walk you home after school?"

"I guess so."

"Cool!"

"I can't wait for my mom to see your braces, Eric."

The walk home passed much too quickly.

"Hey, Mom. Come here. Look at Eric."

"And you worried about what he would think about your braces. Didn't I tell you God has a way of working things out?"

"Aw, Mom. You're not supposed to tell everything."

"You mean, you worried about what I'd think?" Eric asked.

"Yeah. Hey, Mom! Eric wants to know if I can go to a middle school skating party at his church's gym this Friday. Can I go, Mom? Can I?"

Altered Plans

It had been a few years since Red had retired from his teaching position at the university. For Red, retirement did not mean a life spent clutching a remote control. Red was retired, not dead. God still needed Red to use the gifts and talents He had given him.

Many times each year, Red and his wife Roberta took off in their motor home. Each trip was part vacation and part serving God through serving others in whatever way God needed them at that time.

Sometimes their trips took them to places where Red was to speak, an area where God had gifted Red. Other times God used Red's skills to do some work at a church camp or to do repairs in a church that could not afford to pay someone for the upkeep of the church.

So many people were helped by the work Red and Roberta did in their community, but more than that, they were blessed by Red and Roberta's presence. God must have been pleased with Red and Roberta, because they blessed people wherever they went.

On one such trip, Red and Roberta had mapped out their itinerary. They planned a trip south where they were going to spend a little time resting and relaxing with some other retired people in a motor home park before heading for a speaking engagement. When they finished there, Red and Roberta were to make their way most of the way across the country to do some work at a church camp. Red's ministry knew no boundaries. Sometimes God sent Red out of the country to do His work.

Red and Roberta left their home feeling that they knew the work that God had intended for them to do over the next few weeks. God had other plans, because there were people who needed Red more than those whom he had intended to help.

After a two day drive, Red and Roberta arrived at their motor home park and began to unload the car they towed behind them. That is when Red and Roberta's plans began to change. Trying to carry more than he should have, Red had his arms piled so high that he did not see the uneven ground ahead of him. Supplies went everywhere. Red's scream alerted Roberta that all was not right with her husband.

X-rays revealed what Red already knew. The doctor came in to inform Red and Roberta that Red needed surgery. Because of the multiple fractures of his leg and Red's advancing age, his rehabilitation would take quite some time.

Almost immediately, God began to use Red in a new way. Before being sedated prior to surgery, Red prayed for all of those who would be assisting in the operation.

The surgical team had never experienced a patient praying for them before, but then the surgical team had never operated on Red.

Red's prayer before sedation was only the beginning. God revealed to Red the needs of those who were there to meet his needs. God used Red to pray for, hug on, and shed a few tears with those who needed God's comfort.

God sent Red a nurse much too stressed from the rigors of her job. God used Red's prayers and kind words for that nurse to bring about a sense of peace that she had never known.

Red shared God's love with a doctor who needed a large dose of it. Red's doctor was dealing with the stress of a rigorous operating schedule, but he was dealing with much more than that. The doctor's wife had recently decided to call it quits on their marriage and took their son and moved out. Coupled with the burden of burying one of his parents only a few weeks before, this doctor had more than he could handle without God's help.

As word of Red's ministry spread throughout the hospital, many hospital personnel came to visit Red with prayer requests, to seek a few kind words, or to spend some time with a brother in Christ.

Over a period of several weeks, Red learned what many people never learn. Red learned that he did not have to be able to move from one location to another in order to serve God. He only had to be tuned in to where and how God was at work and in what way God wanted Red to help.

While Red ministered to the medical staff, those in the motor home community ministered to Roberta. Red had always assumed the responsibilities for the upkeep on the motor home. Roberta knew nothing about maintaining a motor home. Many of the others in the motor home community helped Roberta in whatever way she needed help. Not only did Roberta feel God's love, but the love of a group of people who were strangers to her only a few weeks before.

Red did not get to do the work that he had set out to do, but he did the work God had intended for him to do. Because of Red, some medical personnel were able to rest a little easier. Because of Red's physical condition, Roberta was able to experience God's love in a way she never expected. Because of a broken leg, many people were able to stop and rest and abide in the love of Jesus Christ. As Red's leg healed, so did the hearts of many who would have never met Red and Roberta if not for some uneven ground.

A Mountaintop Experience

Some people start out the year by making New Year's resolutions. Others watch football games. Brad does neither. Each year Brad starts his year doing something that gets the guys at the office talking.

"You're doing what for New Year's?" one co-worker asked, causing others to chime in.

"Going camping?"

"In a tent?"

"In the mountains?"

"In January? What's wrong with you, anyway? You got a death wish?"

But every year Brad began his year the same way. Just Brad, a tent, and all the provisions he needed, and a few more, just in case. Plus Brad took his "necessary camping equipment."

Before Brad left home, he grabbed his Bible and his journal. Camping in the mountains in the middle of the winter brought Brad closer to God. He cherished his time alone with God.

Brad planned his routine, but there was nothing routine about it. Each morning, Brad woke up and lay in his insulated sleeping bag and listened to the silence or the sounds of nature. Then he got up and read a Psalm.

Brad thought nothing equaled a tent in the mountains when it came to reading Psalms. He got to spend time alone with God and a few of His creatures undisturbed by the breakneck speed of the world.

After reading a Psalm, Brad took a short hike. Sometimes he ran into one of God's creatures -- or at least the tracks that showed one had passed that way.

Somewhere along the trail Brad stopped and reflected on what he saw and how closely it related to what David and others wrote about in Psalms.

After hiking, Brad came back, fixed his breakfast and lay back and let it settle. Then he read another Psalm and let it settle, too.

Then, Brad took out his journal and wrote down his thoughts. Brad continued this for a week, or however long it took him to get through the entire book of Psalms. Brad never hurried to get through by a certain time. Nothing about the mountains said "hurry."

When Brad returned to work, the guys razzed him about his trip. Brad just shook his head with sadness. No one else seemed to realize what they had missed.

Amy's Promise

As Amy stood in the back of the church she thought about the promise she had made to her dad four years before. The time had come to fulfill that promise. Amy stood there alone, but she was not really alone. Her dad was with her.

As the music played and Amy began her walk down the aisle, tears flowed down her cheeks. She closed her eyes for a moment and pictured her dad walking beside her. She thought of the strong man who watched her grow up, not the frail body that lay on the bed dying of cancer to whom she had made her promise.

"Dad, you're the only man in my life, but when I find another man, the man of my dreams with whom I'll spend the rest of my life, you'll walk down the aisle with me and give me away."

Amy clutched the 11" x 14" portrait of her dad tightly with both hands, and it seemed to embrace her as if to give her support. Only a few minutes before, Amy sat and looked at that portrait, one of many pictures her mom and dad had had made when they posed for the new church directory just a few short months before he got sick.

Amy was an only child. She lived where there were few other children to play with. Amy spent a lot of time with her mom and dad. She did not wait until her dad got sick to tell him how much she loved him. Amy told her parents every day, and her mom and dad were quick to tell her the same. When Amy became a teenager and began to date, she never left home without hugging and kissing her mom and dad and telling them how much she loved them.

Amy almost forgot about all the other people in the church that day. It was her moment to spend one more time with her dad. As her tears continued to flow, Amy was sure her dad was shedding a few tears, as well. Amy knew her dad was proud of her choice of Brian for a husband. In many ways Brian reminded Amy of her dad.

Amy met Brian just a few months after her dad passed away. His family moved into town and began attending the same church she did. At first, Brian was just a friend, but as the weeks passed, it became obvious that Brian had become much more than a friend.

As Amy's thoughts moved from her dad to Brian, she looked up at Brian and smiled. If her tears had not been obstructing her focus, she would have noticed that Brian, too, shed a few tears. Amy neared the front of the church, but before she and Brian exchanged vows, there was one other thing she wanted to do.

She looked up at her mother sitting there with her husband Fred. Fred and Amy's mother had been married a year. Amy could see why her mother fell in love with Fred, because Amy had fallen in love with him, too. In a way it was hard for Amy not to ask Fred to walk her down the aisle, but Fred understood the promise she had made to her father.

As Amy drew close to her mother and Fred, she turned and embraced her mother. Then Amy reached over and hugged Fred and gave him a kiss on the top of his bald head, to let everyone know that she loved him, too.

Amy stood up and walked over to Brian and the pastor. Amy still clutched her dad's picture. The pastor began the ceremony and when he got to "Who gives this woman to be married to this man?" just as if her dad was there to answer, Amy turned and sat down her dad's picture.

Every Christmas

Just before November turned into December everyone on Craig and Jennifer's street either jumped for joy or dreaded the occasion because Craig and Jennifer's house was about to undergo a dramatic transformation.

Many of Craig and Jennifer's neighbors decorated for Christmas, but Craig and Jennifer *decorated*. Craig put Santa and all of his reindeer across his roof and a nativity scene under the dogwood tree in the front yard. He installed more lights than the local ballpark. Craig's lights displayed much more color than those at the ballpark.

"Check it out, Jennifer. Do you think we have everything ready?"

"Let me see. Yeah,...I think so. At least as far as I can tell."

"Have we got everything we need for the kids?"

"I think so. We ordered extras this year."

"It was so exciting to have more kids last year than usual. I can't wait until Saturday night."

"Me, either. Have you tried on your suit to make sure it still fits okay?"

"Yeah, how about you? Does your suit still fit?"

"Like a glove. Maybe a little too much like a glove, but I can move around in it okay."

Not only did Craig and Jennifer decorate, but they played Santa and Mrs. Claus for all the children who came. Not only did some of the parents in the neighborhood bring their children, but people came from all over town and even a few came from nearby towns.

Craig and Jennifer did not play Santa and Mrs. Claus only once, they did it three times each week, from 6:00-8:00 p.m. They began the Saturday after Thanksgiving and continued until Christmas Eve.

Finally, the first Saturday night arrived. So did the crowds.

"Ho! Ho! Ho! And how are you, little girl?"

"Fine!"

"And what is your name?"

"Katie."

"Well, that sure is a pretty name for such a pretty little girl. Would you like to tell Santa what you want for Christmas?"

"Didn't you get my letter, Santa?"

"Oh, sure, but I want you to *tell* me, too. That's okay, isn't it?"

"Sure, Santa. I would like a Pretty Princess doll for me and a baseball glove for my little brother."

"And have you been a good little girl this year, Katie?"

"Don't you know?"

"Sure I do, Katie, but I want to know what you think."

"Well...most of the time."

"Well, keep being good, Katie, and I'll come and see you on Christmas Eve. Now, if you'll hop down and go over there to Mrs. Claus, she has a present for you."

"If I take it, will I still get something for Christmas?"

"Sure you will, Katie. Now give Santa a big hug and let Mrs. Claus give you your gift."

Each night Craig and Jennifer gave out gifts and hugs until the last child had been served. Over the course of the holiday season over 700 children received the same gifts from Craig and Jennifer.

When each child tore open the shiny red package he or she found a Christmas stocking full of candy and a little book that told the story of Jesus. Inside the book they found a handwritten message that read: "Santa Claus comes but once a year, but Jesus is with you every day of your life."

Craig and Jennifer continued playing Santa and Mrs. Claus for years until Craig died unexpectedly. Two days after he died, when it was time for visitation at the funeral home, several hundred children and adults showed up carrying Christmas stockings. That Christmas hundreds more showed up at Jennifer's home. Most of them brought Christmas presents.

The following year, as Jennifer was beginning to decorate for Christmas, the doorbell rang. When Jennifer went to answer it, she noticed a young lady whose face looked familiar.

"I know you, don't I? You were here last year! And you were one of our kids!" Jennifer said, becoming more excited with each word.

"That's right. I'm Jessica. My sisters and I came here for years, and I even brought my baby two years ago. Craig's two-and-a-half now. I just found out the other day I'm pregnant again. Naturally, if this one's a girl, we're going to name her Jennifer."

"Please come in, Jessica," Jennifer said, barely able to speak.

"I've just got a minute, but I wanted to give you this."

Jennifer reached out and took the large package from the young woman.

"Goodbye, and Merry Christmas!" Jessica called out as she turned and headed back down the walk to the young man and little boy waiting for her in a SUV parked in front of the house.

Jennifer put down the package, closed the door, and wiped the tears from her cheeks. Then she opened the package to find a framed picture of Jesus with little children sitting at His feet. Also inside the package was a handwritten note, which said, "Jesus loves me this I know, for the Bible tells me so. Thanks for being the first to share Jesus with me. Love, Jessica."

The First Day

The thought of the first day of school frightened Kelly. College meant a lot of changes. As Kelly's first day at college moved along, one professor dashed all hopes Kelly had of remaining unnoticed.

"Class, I would like for each of you to turn around and meet the person behind you and find out about them. Then I want you to find out who is their best friend, and why."

Nervously, Kelly turned around and fell into the most beautiful pair of baby blues she had seen. They came with a smile that matched.

"Hi, I'm Kevin," said the baby blues.

"Oh, uh, hi, I'm Kelly."

"Freshman?" Kevin asked.

"Yeah, is it that obvious? I assume you're not a freshman."

"Sophomore. And don't worry, it's not as bad as you suspect," Kevin assured her.

"It is that obvious," Kelly said.

"Well, kind of. So, ladies first. Who's your best friend?"

"You're gonna laugh," Kelly said.

"No, I promise," Kevin assured her.

Already Kelly felt a little more comfortable.

"My best friend is my mom."

"I think that's cool."

Somehow, Kevin's response did not surprise Kelly.

"I can talk to my mom about everything. I have no secrets from her. And my second best friend is my dad. I wouldn't tell just anyone this, but in a way it was hard for me to leave home. Well, so much for me. Who's your best friend?"

"Now, you're gonna laugh," Kevin said.

"I promise I won't either. Don't tell me it's your mom?"

"No, it's Jesus," Kevin replied.

A lump formed in Kelly's throat as she said, "Now, I think that's cool."

"Really?" Kevin asked.

"I like a guy who's big enough to admit something like that."

"It's hard for me to remember when I didn't know Jesus," Kevin began. "Even as a kid, Jesus was important to me. Just like you are with your mom, I can talk to Jesus about anything. That way I never end up doing anything I regret later. I know how that must sound. I'm not saying I'm perfect, but I try my best to be. Now, you're crying."

"Sorry, I just never expected to meet anyone like you."

"That's okay, I was here all last year and I never met anyone like you," Kevin replied.

"Is anyone looking at me?" Kelly asked.

"No, you're safe. Anyway, it doesn't matter if they are. By the way, there's a Christian fellowship group that meets tonight. As a matter of fact, they've asked me to share what being a Christian means to me. Would you like to go with me and then maybe go out and grab something to eat afterwards?"

"I'd love to."

The Stained Glass Life

Pastor Bill sat hunched over his desk with his eyes focused on his computer screen when a knock at the door interrupted his thoughts.

"Come in," he called out. "Hi, Meagan. It's good to see you," Pastor Bill said as he got up to greet the statuesque freckle-faced redheaded girl.

"Hi, Pastor Bill. It's always good to see you. Thanks for taking the time to talk with me."

"Meagan, I always have time to talk with you. It's been a joy seeing you grow up in this church. Why it seems like only yesterday that your mother had to chase after you as you crawled under pew after pew. I can still remember how your daddy would throw his head back and laugh every time you did that."

"You're embarrassing me, Pastor Bill."

"Sorry about that, Meagan, but I love reliving happy memories. So, what can I do for you today?"

"Well, I just needed someone to talk to, and with Momma spending all her time nursing Daddy back to health after his fall, I figured she has enough to deal with and so I thought of you."

"I'm glad you did, Meagan."

"Pastor Bill, I'm scared. In a few weeks I'll be graduating from college. I'm scared that I'm not cut out to be a teacher, that I might not get hired, and even if I do, that the money will not be enough to pay my bills. I've got no prospects for a husband, and I know Momma and Daddy don't have any extra money to bail me out right now. Is something wrong with me?"

"No, Meagan. These thoughts are quite common to someone in your position. Come on, let's take a walk out to the sanctuary.

"Meagan, when someone needs to talk, I love to bring them out here."

"I can see why. This place is just so peaceful."

"Let's take a seat in the front pew. Look up and tell me what you see."

"You mean the pulpit?"

"No. What else do you see?"

"Well, I see the beautiful stained-glass window."

"Tell me about the stained-glass window, Meagan."

"I don't know what there is to tell. All I can say is it's beautiful. I love to get in here a little early on Sunday morning and just look at it."

"Let me tell you a little story, Meagan. When I was a kid, someone gave me a kaleidoscope and sometimes I held it up to the light and just sat and turned it and looked at all the beautiful pictures it made from little pieces of broken glass. The stained-glass window is a lot like the kaleidoscope."

"You mean all those colorful pieces of broken glass?"

"Yes. Meagan, someone took those colorful pieces of broken glass and put them together to make a work of art. As a teacher, each day you will find many colorful pieces of broken glass sitting in front of you in your classroom. Have you ever thought of how many children are growing up today who are not blessed with two loving parents the way you have been?"

"Well, I think of how lucky I am to have two wonderful parents, but I can't say I've thought much about those who don't have the kind of parents I have."

"Meagan, you can't imagine what some of these kids have to deal with each day, and you have the opportunity to be the artist who blends them together. You've shared with me about your relationship with God, but for some of these kids you'll be the only one they'll ever see who has a relationship with Jesus Christ. Now, with the things the way they are in the school systems today, you can't talk to them about Jesus, but you can tell them how special they are."

"I see what you mean, Pastor Bill."

"Now, let's look at your stained-glass window. The church's stained-glass window looks more beautiful when the light shines through it. Always remember how much you need the Light to make your broken glass beautiful."

"You mean Jesus?"

"Yes, I mean Jesus. All of us have to become broken to Jesus. Then He can heal us. You're scared, but Jesus doesn't want you to be scared. Satan does. Jesus wants you to stand in the Light and He wants you to share His Light with others. Don't worry about what may go wrong. Think of all of those Jesus will send your way. You can bring a little bit of light into their dark world. Now's the time for you to get excited about all of the new opportunities God is giving you. It's not the time to worry about what might go wrong. Don't get me wrong. Not everything will go right all of the time, but when something does go wrong, He'll be there to help you."

"I feel a lot better now. I'm sure glad I came to see you."

"I'm glad you came, too. Feel free to come back any time. Now, let's go to the altar and kneel and pray and see what God has to say to us today."

Strike Three

"Strike three!" the umpire yelled.

Bobby dejectedly looked down at his feet and then looked up to see his best friend Jason, who had been the potential tying run. Jason jogged in from second base.

"Snap out of it, Bobby," Jason said as he arrived at home plate. "We'll get them next time. Let's go get something to eat."

Jason had been a real friend to Bobby even before Bobby was torn apart by the fighting and then separation of his parents.

"Sorry, I can't today," Bobby replied. "I promised Mom I'd go somewhere with her and Tony."

"Later, then," Jason replied, as he turned and walked away.

"Hey, Bobby!"

Bobby turned to see Tony, his mother's boyfriend, calling to him from the other side of the screen. Tony motioned for Bobby to meet him at the end of the dugout.

"It's okay. These things happen," Tony said as he put his arm around Bobby's shoulder.

"I don't mean to be disrespectful, Tony, but are you just saying this to get on my good side because you like my mom?"

"No, Bobby. I guess you could say I'm just saying it so you will realize that God is on your side whether you strike out or hit a home run."

"Tony, do you really think God cares whether I win or lose?"

"Bobby, I don't think God cares whether your team wins or loses, but I do think He cares about whether you win or lose," Tony answered.

"I don't understand," Bobby replied.

"It's like this, Bobby. God really cares about you. He wants to have a relationship with you. He wants to share in your victories, like when you hit a home run, and He wants to comfort you when you strike out. He wants you to spend time with Him no matter how you're feeling."

"Well, I'm feeling pretty rotten right now, and the way things are going, I doubt if I ever hit a home run."

"Bobby, you'll hit some home runs in life. They may or may not be in baseball, but you'll hit some home runs."

"Tony, you're nothing like my dad. In some ways I'm glad Mom and Dad split up. My dad was always embarrassing me. He'd yell at the umpires when things didn't go our way, and then he'd yell at me when I did something wrong. The more he yelled, the more I did wrong. I hated him for that. Particularly when he did it in front of my teammates. I'm still not sure about you, Tony, but I like the fact that you try to cheer me up instead of put me down."

"Bobby, I don't want to talk about your dad, but I do want you to know that I care about you. I think you're a great kid...I mean, young man. I just want you to know that you're special, even when you strike out. Bobby, everyone will be there for you when you hit a home run, but your real friends will also be there when you strike out."

"You mean, like Jason?"

"Yeah, like Jason, and like Jesus. Now come on. Your mom's waiting for us in the car. How does pizza sound?"

Love, Honor, And Obey God

Josh had been looking forward to a special moment in his life for quite a while. He knew he loved Jennifer and he knew she loved him. Josh felt it was time to ask Jennifer to marry him.

Josh had known Jennifer since they were children. At first, Jennifer was merely a girl to him, and Josh had no interest in girls at that early age.

As they grew, Josh learned that girls were cool and that Jennifer was one of the coolest. At first they were friends, but then their friendship grew into something greater.

It made things easier that Josh's parents and Jennifer's parents were good friends, and Josh felt their friendship was strong enough to withstand the test of becoming in-laws.

Josh told his parents what he planned to do. Then he confided in Jennifer's parents. All four parents were excited to hear the good news. Then, it came time to get Jennifer's permission.

As far as Jennifer knew, both families had only gotten together that night for the same reason they had gotten together many times before, good food and fellowship.

Josh had made his and Jennifer's parents promise him that they would not open the door when he took Jennifer out on the front porch, nor would they peer through the blinds to see how Josh was doing.

Finally, Josh got Jennifer away from the others and as they sat on the porch swing, Josh nervously scooted back and forth.

"Is something bothering you, Josh?"

"What makes you think that, Jenn?"

"You just seem a little nervous tonight."

"Well, I am a little nervous tonight, Jenn. There's something I want to ask you."

"If it's what I think it is, the answer is yes."

"And what makes you think you know what I'm going to ask?" Josh asked Jennifer with a grin on his face.

"Maybe because everyone's been wondering forever when you'd get up the courage. Some people have even made bets about it," Jennifer answered.

"Oh, they have, have they? Well, it's not going to be as easy on you as you think, Jenn. There are conditions, you know."

"Oh, there are, huh? And what are the conditions?"

"Jenn, I need for you to be serious for a moment. Okay?"

"Believe me, I am serious," Jennifer answered, still smiling.

"Jenn, I mean it. Don't get me mixed up, now. The real thing is not as easy as I rehearsed it. I even have to have notes."

"You rehearsed this? And you have notes? You didn't by any chance make a tape of it, did you, Josh?"

"Come on, Jenn. If you don't cooperate, this will take all night."

"Okay, Josh. I'll be quiet. Go ahead. Hey! Who's that looking out the blinds?"

"They promised me they wouldn't!"

"So, you did talk to the old folks first."

"Yeah, but they told me they wouldn't spy on us."

"There's nobody spying on us. I was just seeing what you'd say. Now, will you go ahead before you go down in history as the first person to make a two day marriage proposal."

"Okay, Jenn. As always, you've seen right through me. I love you and I want to marry you, but before you answer, I want to tell you what the conditions are. Jenn, don't cry. You'll make me cry."

"I'm sorry, Josh. It's just that I'm so happy, and you know me, I only have two sides of my personality, cut up or extremely serious. By the way, Josh. I'm impressed. You asked me to marry you, and you didn't have to look at your notes once."

"Okay, Jenn. Go back to crying so I can continue."

"The conditions, Josh?"

"First, Jenn, I want you to know that you'll never be first in my life."

72

"I already know that, Josh. One reason I love you so much is that you put God before anything or anyone."

"That's right, Jenn. I want you to know that we need to put God before any relationship, activity, achievement, or possession."

"I totally agree, Josh."

"Jenn, not only do we need to give our hearts to God, but we need to give Him our wills, our minds, our bodies, our finances, and our future."

"Oh, Josh! I love you so much! Of course, I'll marry you! And of course I'll agree to all those things. You know I believe in the same things you do. Our parents brought us up right, Josh. God is first. Everything else comes after Him."

"Whew! I'm glad all that's over with. Give me a kiss and then we can go tell the folks."

"Okay, Josh. I can't wait to tell them how hard it was for me to keep from laughing every time you looked at your notes."

Christmas Vacation

Jim had worked at his job long enough that he received four weeks vacation each year, but it was how he spent one week in early December that made him appreciate the other fifty-one.

Anxious to begin his journey, Jim laced up his uncomfortable shoes that were one size too small. He had almost forgotten what it was like to have one sole flap as he walked, while the hole in the other one let him know each time he stepped in a puddle of water.

"I'd better go now. I've got a long walk ahead of me," Jim told his wife and kids as he kissed them goodbye and turned to leave.

As the wind cut through him, Jim picked up the pace. He had no idea what time he would get to town because town was at least three hours away. It was almost twelve miles to town, and while Jim exercised regularly, he did not do it in twelve mile increments that often. Actually, he did it only once a year.

The first night was always the toughest for Jim, because he did not get to town until after dark and by then all the good places to stay were already taken. The temperature plummeted as darkness fell and the unlined old overcoat Jim wore made him long for his comfortable home and cozy bed.

Just as Jim expected, he had trouble finding somewhere to stay. It was then that Jim had an idea.

"No one goes to the waterfront this time of year unless they have to. It's much colder. I bet I can find a place there," Jim thought to himself as he hurried to see what he could find.

After searching a few minutes for something to protect him from the elements, Jim found a discarded large cardboard box. The box was a little damp, but Jim could not be too choosy on his first homeless night. Jim braced the box against a building as best he could to keep the effects of the wind at a minimum.

First nights were always the toughest for Jim. First nights always made him have second thoughts.

As Jim braced the box against a wall and was about to turn in for the night he spotted another man coming his way.

"That box looks big enough for two. Mind sharing it with me? I'll share my can of beans with you," the other man said.

"I could use something to eat," Jim replied. "You've got a deal!"

The man's odor told Jim that this was not the other man's first homeless night. Still, Jim agreed to the offer. Besides, two men in a box stay warmer than one. Jim had forgotten all about food in his haste to find lodging, and he knew that the other man would have trouble finding another place with any protection from the elements.

The beans and the long walk made Jim sleepy, so after a little conversation, he dozed off. He only woke up once during the night, and after remembering where he was and seeing that his companion remained with him, he soon fell back to sleep.

Jim awakened early the next morning to the sound of river traffic and found his boxmate had checked out early. Soon, he found himself third in line at the back door of a nearby restaurant to take whatever table scraps were offered. It was not a lot, but he would make do. It would not be many days until his life would return to normal. His companions did not have such a sunny forecast.

After cramming the food into his mouth and being careful not to drop any, he left as the others did to begin a day of walking, standing, and sitting, an itinerary that made the day seem much longer.

Some of the homeless headed for heated buildings, but not Jim. He had those anytime, only he would appreciate them more the following week.

"Got any change so a fellow could get something to eat and a cup of coffee?" Jim asked a passerby.

Some gave Jim their loose change. Others refused. Jim knew many refused because they expected him to use it to buy alcohol.

Jim disliked panhandling but realized it was a once a year thing for him. Many had to do it every day to get by. Jim panhandled enough to get a cup of coffee and a small lunch and realized he would have to do it again if he expected any supper.

On his second night, Jim secured a better spot for sleeping. The alley he chose was protected on three sides from the wind.

When Jim awoke early the next morning, he got up and headed to the waterfront to wash. It was Sunday and Jim was going to the local mission to worship. Sunday was Jim's favorite homeless day. Not only did the sermon warm him inside, but so did the hot meal the mission provided after the service.

As the week wore on, Jim adjusted to the elements. At least he adjusted to some of them. While the nights did not seem as cold, the ground did seem harder. At last, Jim had survived another week and had renewed an appreciation for all that God had given him.

Jim's smile seemed out of place among the waterfront crowd. Jim was going somewhere none of the others were going. He was going home to a loving family and a warm house, and to try to figure out why God had chosen to bless him instead of one of those he had encountered during his homeless week.

Every Friday

"Do you think he'll come today?"

"It's Friday, isn't it?"

"What are you two talking about?"

"The man who comes to see Charlie. He's the only one who's ever been here to see Charlie. Charlie's wife died a few years ago and his son was killed in Vietnam. As far as anyone knows they were the only family Charlie ever had."

"Then who's this guy? And why does he come to the nursing home each week and sit and feed Charlie when everyone knows that Charlie can't recognize anyone anymore?"

"That's what I've been wondering. I think I've finally gotten up enough nerve to ask him when he comes today."

"Well, now's your chance, because here he comes."

Down the hall walked a well-dressed man who appeared to be in his fifties. The spring in his step showed that he was happy to be there.

"How are you today, sir?"

"Fine, nurse. And yourself?"

"Couldn't be better."

"Me, either," the man replied as he continued down the hall to Charlie's room.

"I thought you said you were going to ask him," Danielle, the young nurse, said to Margaret.

"I'm going to ask him, but I'm going to wait until he leaves. Don't let him get past me."

"I won't! I want to know, too!"

Margaret headed down the hall. As she passed Charlie's room she heard the stranger say, "You're looking good today, Charlie. I see you're having cream of tomato soup. I know that's one of your favorites."

Margaret headed down the hall checking on each patient's needs. She did her best to see that the mysterious man did not get away before she found out how he was connected to Charlie.

"Margaret!"

Margaret looked up and saw Danielle hurrying toward her.

"Yes, Danielle. What is it?"

"I think he's getting ready to leave."

"Thanks, Danielle. Can you stay with Edith for a few minutes?"

"I'd be happy to."

Margaret headed up the hall and arrived at Charlie's room just as the mysterious man walked out.

"You have a good weekend, nurse."

"You, too, sir. By the way, sir. Some of us are curious about something."

"You want to know my connection to Charlie. Right?"

"How did you guess?"

"Well, it's no secret that Charlie has no family left."

"I hope you don't mind me asking."

"Not at all. Actually, I have two connections to Charlie. First of all, Charlie's son saved my life in Vietnam. He pushed me out of the way of a sniper's bullet and ended up taking the bullet himself. I had trouble living with that. I came home and got a job, but I turned to drugs, lost my job, and all my family disowned me."

"And Charlie took you in?"

"In a way, but not exactly. I ended up on the streets and then at a homeless shelter. Every Friday, Charlie came to the homeless shelter and served lunch. Not only did he serve us lunch, but he talked to us like we were just as good as he was. I found out his name and put two and two together. When I told Charlie that his son Jerry saved my life in Vietnam, he began to treat me like a son. He helped me clean up my act and find the Lord. He even helped me get a job.

"I got a promotion and moved away, but Charlie and I kept in touch. When his wife died, I took some time off work and came back for her funeral.

"After a while I didn't hear from Charlie any more. I didn't know what happened to him. Finally, I was able to find out that Charlie had had a stroke. I knew Charlie didn't have anyone to take care of him, so I managed to get a job transfer to a city nearby. Since I work a four day work week, I have Fridays off. Now I can do for Charlie what he did for me."

"And for me and a lot of others."

"Huh? I don't understand."

"You say you're a Christian. Surely you know the story of the one leper who went back and thanked Jesus. Not only do I think of you as the leper who went back and thanked Jesus, but one who went and served in the leper colony, as well. Stories such as yours inspire people to go and do likewise. I'm off on Tuesdays. Edith doesn't have anyone, either. I bet she could use a lunchtime companion."

Trading Licks

Joey skipped over and hopped up on a bench near the door leading to the courtroom. Joey squirmed back and forth until he got comfortable and then he began to look around. Not far away two deputies stood guarding the courtroom door. On a bench across the way Mrs. Humphries sat working a crossword puzzle while she kept watch on Joey out of the corner of her eye. Mrs. Humphries lived next door to Joey. She had promised Joey's mother that she would watch him so that his mother could go in and observe the trial.

Joey looked back and forth at the passersby and occasionally traded grins with Mrs. Humphries. After a while he leaned over to one side so that he could pull a sucker from his jeans pocket. After a little twisting and turning, he successfully grasped his candy treat. He took off the red paper and popped it into his mouth.

Joey looked over and noticed another little boy turn away from the water fountain. Water dripped from his chin. The second boy headed in Joey's direction.

"Hi," the other boy said.

"Hi," Joey replied.

"What've you got in your mouth?" the other boy asked.

"A sucker. You want a lick?" Joey asked.

"Sure!" the other boy answered.

"You like it?" Joey asked as the other boy removed it from his mouth and handed it back to Joey.

"Yeah. What kind is it?"

"It's cherry," Joey answered. "Cherry's my favorite kind. What's your favorite?"

"Grape," the other boy answered. "But I like cherry, too."

"Want another lick?" Joey asked.

"Sure!" the other boy answered.

For the next several minutes the two boys sat beside each other on the bench taking turns licking the sucker and then handing it to the other boy until there was nothing left but the stick.

"You got any more suckers?" the other boy asked.

"Nope," Joey answered. "That was my only one."

"It sure was good, wasn't it?"

"Yeah, and it was even better sharing it with a friend."

"You mean I'm your friend. I never had a friend before," replied the other boy.

"Never had a friend! You've got to be kidding!"

"Nope. You're my first friend."

"See that woman sitting over there?"

"Yeah, what about her?"

"Well, that's Mrs. Humphries. She's my friend, too."

"She's kind of old to be a friend, isn't she?"

"Nope. Friends come in all ages and sizes."

"I didn't know that. I'm sure glad to be your friend."

"Me, too," Joey replied as he scooted over and put his sticky hand around the other boy's shoulder.

For the next few minutes the two boys sat arm in arm. Neither realized that a shared sucker meant less licks for each of them. Neither realized that a shared sucker could have meant germs. And neither realized that on the other side of the wall that one boy's father was on trial for murdering the other boy's father.

Love Thy Neighbor

"Betty, come here quick!"

"What is it, Fred?"

"Look, Betty! Out the window!"

"What are you talking about, Fred? I don't see anything except John mowing the lawn."

"That's what I'm talking about, Betty. You know how much John hates mowing the lawn."

"But he has to mow it sometime, Fred."

"But, Betty! He's mowing *our* lawn!"

"He is, isn't he? You think maybe he's had too much sun and lost his sense of direction?"

"Could be. What do I do, Betty?"

"What do you mean, 'What do I do?'"

"Well, to be honest, I'm torn. I want to go out and make sure he's all right, but then I'm afraid if I do, he'll quit mowing and I'll have to finish it."

"I think you'd better go out and check on John."

"I guess you're right, Betty. By the way, if it turns out he doesn't know what he's doing, do you think you'd like to finish mowing the lawn?"

"Fred!"

"That's what I thought, Betty. Now, where did I put my shoes?"

"You know perfectly well where they are. Now, no more stalling. Get out there and check on John."

Fred opened the patio door and stepped out into the heat.

"Hi, John. It's me. Fred."

"I know perfectly well who you are, Fred. Remember, we've lived next door to each other for eleven years."

"What are you doing, John?"

"What does it look like I'm doing, Fred? I'm mowing the lawn."

"But, John. Do you by any chance realize it's my lawn?"

"Of course I do, Fred. After all, I'm not stupid, you know."

"Oh, now I get it."

"Now you get what, Fred?"

"John, I consider Betty and me to be friends of yours and Marsha's, but there's no way we're getting into that new business of yours."

"What new business, Fred? I don't have any new business."

"You don't?"

"No, I just decided to mow your lawn."

"Yeah, right! Am I supposed to decide to mow your lawn next week?"

"No, Fred."

"So, you want your house painted?"

"No, Fred. I just decided to mow your lawn."

"John, remember how you said we've lived next door to each other for eleven years?"

"Yeah. So?"

"Well, how many times have you mowed my lawn in eleven years?"

"Well, if you'd leave me alone, once."

"My point exactly. What gives?"

"Okay, Fred. I'll come clean. Marsha and I are trying to become the kind of people God calls us to be."

Before Fred could answer, he heard the sliding glass door open and turned and saw Betty.

"Fred!"

"It's not a good time, Betty."

"But, Fred. I need to know if you want to do something tonight."

"Betty, you know we can't. We have kids. Remember?"

"I know, Fred. But Marsha's agreed to baby-sit so we can go out."

"Don't do it, Betty! John and Marsha have joined a cult! Evidently they're going to start by brainwashing our kids. Oh, Betty, all of a sudden we live next door to the pod people!"

83

The Difference Maker

Joeley looked forward to Tuesday nights. Every Tuesday night, people gathered at her house for Bible study. The youth headed to the basement, while the adults met in the family room.

As Joeley sat at the dinner table and looked at her parents, she thought back to two short years before. A stranger made a difference in their lives because he paid them a visit.

"Is your mom or dad at home?" the stranger asked.

"They can't come to the door right now," Joeley replied.

Joeley told the truth. Only minutes before her mom had stormed into the bedroom and locked the door. Almost immediately, Joeley's dad stomped out the back door, slammed it shut, and fumed in the back yard. In those days, tense times outnumbered peaceful ones at Joeley's house.

"Well, I'm from the church down the street. Do you go to church anywhere?" the stranger asked.

"I haven't ever been to church," Joeley replied.

"You haven't! Well, do you have a Bible?"

"No, never had one," Joeley replied.

"Well, I'd like to give you one. Will you promise me you'll read it if I give you one?" the stranger asked.

"I guess so, but I'm not allowed to open the door to strangers."

"How about if I leave it on the porch and you can come out and get it after I leave?"

"I guess that'd be okay."

"Here, I'll mark where to start reading."

"You mean I don't start at the beginning?"

"Not this time."

Joeley never expected that Bible to make a difference in her life. She never expected its message would work miracles in her mom and dad's lives.

Not only did Joeley open the Bible and look through it, she spent most of the night reading it. Somewhere in the middle of the night Joeley fell asleep, but she finished most of the book of John before her head dropped and her eyes closed.

Overcome by her emotions at school the next day, Joeley decided to confide in her best friend.

"Can we talk?" Joeley asked.

"Of course. Anytime. What's your problem?"

Joeley shared her predicament and her plan with her friend.

"Let's pray," Joeley's friend suggested. Joeley and her friend prayed right in the middle of the hall between classes.

At dinner that night, before her parents could get involved in another argument, Joeley gathered enough courage to speak.

"A stranger left this on our doorstep yesterday. I've been reading it, but I think the two of you need it more than I do."

She laid the Bible on the table and continued. "It's no fun growing up in a house where you two are always arguing. What has happened to the two of you? You used to love each other."

Before her parents could answer, Joeley bounded from the table and headed to her room. She wanted to take her Bible but hoped leaving it behind would do more good.

After Joeley left the room, Richard and Karen looked at the Bible laying on the table and then looked up at one another as tears streamed from their eyes.

Richard reached down and picked up the Bible and walked around the table. He put his arm around his wife and held her tight.

"Let's try again," Richard said. "And let's use this book for advice."

Teary-eyed, Karen could only nod her head.

That Sunday, Joeley and her mom and dad visited the church up the street, and neither of her parents noticed that the pastor shed a tear when they walked in the door.

The Good Samaritan Pick-Up

Seldom did Mike stop to help stranded motorists, but once he made an exception. Mike had no idea that the stranded motorist was a gorgeous, long-legged redhead. It was too dark to tell who sat behind the wheel. However, as soon as he spotted the stalled vehicle, he remembered the story of The Good Samaritan.

Only a few nights before, Mike was alone in a motel room with nothing to do. He slid open the desk drawer and spotted a Bible. He had read a Bible as a child, and he decided to open it and see what it held for him as an adult. Maybe if he had not done so, he would not have stopped for the stranded motorist.

But Mike did stop, and he got out to see if he could help. Little did he know his soon-to-be acquaintance could help him, as well.

"Got a problem?" Mike asked.

"If I didn't need help, I would try to think of a smart answer to such a dumb question, like, 'No, I always pull over to the side of the road to see who might stop for me.'"

"I guess it was a dumb question at that. Let me try another one. Do you have any idea what's wrong?"

"Actually, yes, and now it's my time to be the dumb one. I ran out of gas."

"Doesn't your gas gauge work?"

"It does, but my mind was on the great time I had tonight. I had been too rushed earlier to take the time to fill it up."

"Would I be too nosy if I asked, 'Great time doing what?' I assume you had a date."

"Nothing like that. Tonight was my Bible study night."

"Your Bible study night?"

"That's right! Every Thursday night. You sound surprised. You do know what a Bible study is, don't you?"

"Of course. You just took me by surprise."

"I don't understand."

"Yeah, and I think I might put my foot in my mouth if I explain."

"I like men with dexterity. Go ahead and insert your foot."

"Only if you promise not to get mad."

"I promise."

"Okay, you just don't seem the type that would be involved in a Bible study."

"And what type is that?" the redhead asked.

"Someone who can't think of anything else to do," Mike replied.

"In other words, you think Bible study is for losers?" she shot back.

"No, I just associate Bible study with homely types," Mike replied.

"Have you ever been to a Bible study?"

"No."

"Would you be willing to try one one time to see what you think?"

"I don't know. See, I don't really know a lot about the Bible."

"That sounds like a good reason to go to Bible study."

"Your husband doesn't mind you asking other men to go to Bible study?"

"Are you asking that question to see what my husband thinks or are you trying to find out if I have a husband?"

"Truth?" Mike asked.

"Truth," the redhead replied.

"Actually, to see if you have a husband."

"No ring. No husband. You know how us Bible study types are. Too homely to catch anyone's eye. Now, are you willing to give a Bible study a try?"

"I'll make you a deal. You give dinner a try one night and I'll give Bible study a try."

"I'll tell you what I'll do. I'll meet you somewhere for dinner."

"Deal. And if you run out of gas on the way, I'll come and pick you up."

And A Little Child Shall Lead Them

Some children gag at the announcement of a homework assignment. Not Ricky. Ricky's Sunday school teacher had given his class an assignment, and Ricky intended to carry it out.

"Are you sure this is where you want to go, Ricky?" his mother asked.

"Yeah, this is where God told me to go."

"Okay, then. Do you want me to go with you or wait here?"

"No, this is my job, Mom. You wait here until I get back."

Ricky opened the car door, got out and closed it behind him. Other boys had told Ricky about Mrs. Cummings. Some of them said no one had seen her in years. No one except the boy who delivered her groceries. Others said she stayed drunk most of the time. Ricky suspected his friends made up much of these rumors in order to scare him.

Ricky climbed the steps one at a time, opened the outside door of the apartment house, and stepped inside. Each step led him closer to another floor. The closer he got to the top floor, the more scared he became.

As Ricky turned on the staircase halfway between the fifth and sixth floor, each squeak made him jump a little more. His feet got heavier with each step.

As Ricky reached Mrs. Cummings's apartment, he hesitated, prayed, then knocked lightly at her door. Afraid that he had wasted his opportunity, he knocked a second time, only louder this time.

In a moment a woman with messed up gray hair opened the door.

"What do you want, little boy?" Mrs. Cummings asked.

Ricky spewed out the words before he lost his courage. "I want you to know that Jesus loves you because my Sunday School teacher told me so, and since Jesus loves you, I want to know if you will go to church with me this morning."

Only the night before, Mrs. Cummings had prayed and asked Jesus if he was real to let her know.

Visibly shaken, Mrs. Cummings asked, "Who...who sent you to see me?"

"Which one would get you to go to church with me? If I tell you my Sunday School teacher did it, or if I say Jesus sent me, because it was kinda both of them?"

"Just wait until I get my shoes on, little boy," Mrs. Cummings said as she tried to hide the tears streaming down her cheeks.

"Okay, but hurry up. My mom's waiting for us in the car."

Mrs. Cummings came back shortly. She had dried her tears, put on her shoes, and combed her hair as best she could.

"Here, take my hand, Mrs. Cummings. These steps are mighty steep and I wouldn't want you to fall on your way to your first day at church."

Grace Multiplied

Lindsey spread out on her dorm room bed stressed by the closeness of finals and the lack of funds she needed to get through the week.

Lindsey needed a break from her studies. She hopped up and checked her purse to see how much money she had left. Four dollars and fifty-eight cents did not sound like a lot of money considering there were three days left before she got paid.

She devised a plan and opted for a trip to the corner market for a loaf of bread and a jar of peanut butter. She grabbed her coat and headed out the door and down the stairs.

Lindsey arrived at Al's Market just before it closed. She checked the prices to make sure she had enough money and headed to the counter with her purchase.

To save a few steps in the biting wind, Lindsey decided to leave by the back door. As she stepped into the alley, she jumped as a nearby noise frightened her.

"Oh, don't be alarmed, Miss. Howie and I were just looking through the garbage cans trying to find something to eat. We won't hurt you."

Lindsey turned to see a couple of elderly men in raggedy clothes. The one who spoke to her tipped his soiled hat and smiled as he spoke.

Lindsey looked at the two men and then at her sack. "I just realized I don't need this. Could you two gentlemen use a loaf of bread and a jar of peanut butter?"

"Could we? Are you sure you don't need it, Miss?"

"Oh, positive. I just realized I already have some at home. Here, take it, and let me see if Al has a knife you can use."

"Why that is very kind of you, Miss. God bless you."

Lindsey reentered the store and talked Al into giving her an old knife. She left again and handed the knife to the homeless man who had spoken to her.

"Here you are. Well, I must be on my way now."

"Thanks again, Miss. You are much too kind."

Lindsey headed out of the alley and back to the dorm. Her heart was full, but her stomach was still empty. She wondered how she would survive the week.

"Excuse me, Miss, but I think you dropped this," said an elderly man as he handed her an envelope.

"Oh, no. This isn't mine," Lindsey replied, as she turned to return the envelope to the elderly gentleman, but he was nowhere in sight.

"Where could he have gone?" Lindsey wondered.

Lindsey opened the envelope and found a note inside.

"For as much as you have done unto the least of these, you have done unto me."

Inside the note Lindsey found two twenty dollar bills upon which she deposited a few tears.

Knocking At The Door

Sandy had just come into the house from the back yard when she heard the doorbell. She smiled as she opened the front door. She looked at the tall, thin, mustachioed man who appeared to be in his mid-thirties, the man who had left her a book only a few days before.

As the door opened, Alan looked at the tall, attractive, auburn-haired young woman standing in the door in front of him. It had been several months since Alan's wife Denise had died. While he had seen many women since then, this was the first time he had paid attention to one. It felt good to see a woman's smile again.

"Please come in," Sandy said, as she held the door open for Alan.

"I hope you've read part of the book," Alan said after entering the house. He was unable to take his eyes off of her green eyes.

"Read it! I devoured it! I read the whole book! It's a wonderful novel! Are you the one who wrote it?"

"Well, I always say that God wrote it. He just lets me pound the keys on the computer."

"Well, you do a wonderful job of pounding, I must say. How many books have you written?"

"Three, so far."

"All of them novels?"

"Yes."

"Are all of them the same series?"

"No, two of them are."

"Do you happen to have copies with you?"

"Well, as a matter of fact, I do. Why do you ask?"

"I can't wait to read more of them. Would you happen to have five copies of each book?"

"You read five copies at once?"

93

"Of course, doesn't everyone?" Sandy answered laughing. "Actually, I'd like a copy for myself, one for my mom, one for my sister, and a couple of each to have on hand in case I want something to give as a gift."

"You didn't even ask how much they are."

"Whatever they are, they're a bargain. Will you take a check?"

"Of course, and I must say I like a high-pressure customer."

Alan went to his car and returned with fifteen books.

"Here you go. Would you like them signed and personalized?"

"I'd like all of them signed and three of each copy personalized, if you don't mind. By the way, I don't mean to be nosy, but was Denise your wife? I saw where your book was dedicated to her memory."

"Yes, she's been gone eight months now. She died just before I sent the last book off to the publisher."

"I'm sorry. I can't begin to imagine how hard it must be on you."

"It's been rough all right, but God is helping me deal with it."

"Please sit down while I write you a check."

After Sandy wrote and handed the check to Alan, they began to talk. Their conversation continued for quite some time. It was obvious that neither Alan nor Sandy were eager to end the visit, but Alan never expected what was to follow.

Alan watched as Sandy got up from her chair, knelt before him, and looked up into his eyes.

"Alan, will you marry me?" Sandy asked.

Alan laughed, and replied, "I thought you'd never ask."

Sandy laughed, too, but something in her demeanor told Alan there was at least a little seriousness in her question.

"You are kidding, aren't you?" Alan asked.

"I'm not sure," Sandy answered. "I'm not ready to marry you, if that's what you want to know, but then I've never met a man quite like you. While I may not be in love with you yet, I definitely fell in 'like' with you as I spent time reading your book."

"Well, I must say, I'm much nicer in my books," Alan replied, and he and Sandy laughed.

Still, Alan could see that Sandy was somewhat serious about all of this.

"Do you have a full-length mirror by any chance?"

Puzzled, and caught off guard, Sandy recovered and replied, "Yes, people as tall as we are definitely need full-length mirrors, don't we? Follow me."

"How's this?" Sandy asked after showing Alan the bathroom. "Sorry, but it's the only one I have."

"This will be fine. Now, stand beside me."

"At five-eleven it feels good to stand beside a man who is taller than I am."

"Maybe, so. But that's not what I'm getting at. Look at the two of us. What do you see?" Alan asked.

"I don't understand," Sandy replied.

"Well, I'll tell you what I see," Alan said. "I see a lanky old man and a beautiful young woman. That's what I see."

"And just how old are you, lanky old man?"

"Thirty-seven."

"Well, I'm twenty-five and I see nothing wrong with twelve years difference in age between two mature people."

"And what about the looks difference?" Alan asked.

"Well, I must say that one of us looks like a man and the other one looks like a woman, but I always thought that kind of difference made the best marriages. I hope you're not saying someone should be interested in someone else strictly based on looks."

"Not at all. I just think you could do better."

"I beg to differ. I'm tired of guys my age. They're so immature and only interested in themselves. The only thing they care about in a woman is her looks and her body. You're not saying that's what you think, too, are you?"

"Absolutely not! I must admit that men notice a woman's looks before they notice anything else, but...well, let's put it this way...I think you're gorgeous, but what makes you stand out is I think you're even more beautiful on the inside."

"That's what I'm getting at. I don't think I've ever met a man like that. Alan, let me try to tell you how I felt when I read your book. You made me laugh. You made me cry. You made me tingle all over. No man has ever done that to me. But most of all, I saw a man who has a special relationship with Jesus Christ. I want to spend the rest of my life with a man like that. Now, what? You're laughing and crying at the same time. What gives?"

"I'm crying because I've felt so lonely these last eight months and now all of a sudden I don't feel lonely anymore. As for why I'm laughing, I was just wondering which would sound better, to tell our kids that we fell in love in the bathroom or to tell them we fell in love looking at ourselves in the mirror."

What's Wrong With Dad?

Kyle looked down at his sleeping dad. As he looked at his dad, Kyle could not help but think of the changes in his dad in the last week. It all began when his dad had knocked on the door of Kyle's room.

"Come in," Kyle answered, not at all expecting what would come next.

"Oh, hi, Dad. Is there something you want?" Kyle asked.

"Yes, Kyle, there is," John answered. "I want to know how you're doing."

"Excuse me, Dad. What did you say?" Kyle asked.

"I said 'I want to know how you're doing,'" John repeated.

"Oh, um, I'm fine, Dad. How are you?" Kyle replied, not knowing what to think of his dad's question.

"No, Kyle. I want to know how you're really doing." John asked his son.

"I'm really doing fine. What's wrong, Dad? You don't have cancer, do you? There's nothing wrong with Mom, is there?"

"No, Son. Everything's fine. I just want to know how you're doing."

"You didn't get transferred, did you, Dad? Tell me you didn't get transferred. I like it here and so does Kelly."

"No, Son. I didn't get transferred."

"Then what gives, Dad?"

"Kyle, I just realized how quickly you're growing up and how soon you and Kelly will be gone and how little time I've spent with you."

"Have you talked to Kelly yet, Dad?"

"No, Kyle. You're the oldest. I wanted to talk to you first."

"Then excuse me a minute, Dad. I'll be back in a minute."

"Where are you going, Son?"

"I just wanted to warn Kelly. That's all. I'm afraid all this sudden love will freak her out, and I want to break the news to her gently."

"Sit down, Kyle. Anyway, Mom's talking to her now."

"You mean Mom's weird now, too."

"We're not weird, Kyle. We've just decided to become the parents we always should've been. That's all."

"Well, Dad, really I'm fine. Really! Oh, now I get it. You saw some commercial on TV about drugs. Don't worry, Dad. Neither Kelly or I are dumb enough to do drugs."

"I don't think either of you are on drugs, Kyle. Can't parents talk to their kids?"

"Don't you remember, Dad? We talked last year on my birthday."

"Yeah, and I'm not sure we've really talked since."

"Well, we have if you count 'pass the potatoes, Son.'"

"That's what I'm talking about. We really haven't spent any time together. I'll tell you what. Do you have plans this Saturday?"

'Uh, why do you ask, Dad?"

"Well, I thought we'd spend some time together."

"You mean it's supposed to rain."

"Why did you say that, Son?"

"Don't you remember, Dad? You always play golf on Saturday."

"Well, this Saturday I won't. This Saturday I'll spend all day with you. We'll do whatever you like as long as I can afford it."

"Dad, you didn't start drinking, did you?"

"No, Son, I didn't start drinking."

"Dad, when is the last time you had your medication checked?"

"Kyle, there's nothing wrong with me. Can't a father do something with his kids every now and then?"

"Oh, I get it now. Your foursome canceled out on you and this is supposed to last us until I go off to college."

"No, Son. I'm serious. I'm really serious."

"I know, and you're freaking me out."

"Son, just trust me. Whatever you want to do, we'll do together Saturday."

"Anything, Dad?"

"As long as I can afford it, Son."

Kyle looked down at his dad. He appeared to be waking up.

"Hi, Dad."

"Hi, Son."

"So you know who I am. You're getting better."

"Yes, Son. The doctor says I'll live."

"Dad, are you mad at me for getting you on those rollerblades?"

"No, son, but don't let me do any more downhills. When I plowed into the Ross's car, I thought I was a goner."

"You almost were, Dad. You almost were."

"So, how's your mom doing?"

"She'll be okay, Dad. Kelly's with her now. It looks like the two of you will be getting released tomorrow."

"What did she do with Kelly?"

"You'd never believe it. Oh, Dad. Kelly and I are so sorry. We didn't really think the two of you would go through with it. Dad, Kelly and I love the two of you."

"Kyle, Mom and I love you and Kelly, too, but remember, no more downhills."

"I promise, Dad. I promise. Hey, Dad! Have you ever tried bungee jumping?"

Dear Diary

Mandy reached the top of the attic steps and spotted her mother sitting on the floor reading something.

"What are you reading, Mom?"

"Oh, nothing, Mandy."

"Mom, it sure looks like something to me. Let me see."

"Okay, but you've got to promise not to laugh."

"I promise, Mom. Aha! So it's your diary!"

"Mandy, you promised you wouldn't laugh."

"So what are you reading?"

"It's what I wrote when I got home from a date one night. Mandy, you promised you wouldn't laugh."

"Okay, Mom, but *this* I've got to read."

"I guess there are some things mothers should share with their daughters."

Mandy took the diary from her mother's hands and began to read the page her mother was reading.

Dear Diary,

Today I fell in love. It was like something in the movies. At first I was sorry that Trish and Becky did not want to ride the rollercoaster with me, but that all changed when I met Bill.

Bill! There was no boy in my school as handsome as Bill. I'll always remember standing in line waiting to ride the rollercoaster. I noticed him right away, but I was afraid he wouldn't notice me.

We were almost ready to get on the coaster when he turned around and saw me, and I will never forget his first words.

"Do you have anyone to ride with?"

I was so nervous all I could do was shake my head.

"Well, would you like to ride with me?"

He probably thought I couldn't talk, when all I could do was nod.

He got on first and then held out his hand to help me in. "What a gentlemen," I thought.

I remember looking over at him and smiling as we slowly climbed the first hill. Then we got to the top. I don't remember what happened next, but Bill told me I screamed as we started going down. I just remember that he gripped my left hand with his right, as an act of gallantry.

He also told me that he grabbed me when we got off in order to steady me because I was walking kind of funny. He must've been right. After all, I'm sure that Bill would never lie.

I guess I'll find out Monday if Trish and Becky still want to be friends, but I didn't really ditch them. I just decided to spend time with Bill.

What fun we had this afternoon sharing the same cotton candy, as he ate from the right side and I ate from the left. And what muscles he must have had to swing that mallet and ring the bell to win that stuffed animal. It's the biggest stuffed animal I've ever seen!

But nothing will equal tonight, especially the Ferris wheel ride. Up and down we went. We watched the park's lights as the wind blew through our hair. But of course, I'll never forget what Bill said when our car stopped on top.

"Carol, you know what they say a boy is supposed to do when he is with a girl and the car stops on top, don't you?"

"No, Bill. What do they say?" I answered flirtatiously.

"They say it's bad luck if the boy doesn't kiss the girl."

"Really," I replied, not knowing if it was the truth or not. "Well, we don't want any bad luck, do we?"

I remember how everyone laughed when we got to the bottom and we were still kissing. I didn't mind. I was kissing *him*.

Mandy was laughing so hard by this time that she had to put down the diary.

"Mandy, you said you wouldn't laugh!"

"But Mom, I didn't know it would be so funny! Did you actually write this stuff?"

"Yes, Mandy, I did."

"Whatever happened to this Bill guy, anyway?"

"What do you mean 'Whatever happened to this Bill guy?' Who do you think that is sitting downstairs in the living room?"

"You mean Dad? That handsome guy with all those muscles is that bald-headed guy with the bulging belly?"

"Well, he's still handsome to me."

"Tell me something, Mom."

"What's that, dear?"

"If you and Dad were on that same Ferris wheel today, would you kiss from the top to the bottom."

"Are you kidding? Your dad would be gasping for breath before we were a third of the way down. But, you know what?"

"What's that, Mom?" Mandy asked as a grin spread across her face.

"Every time your dad gives me a peck on the lips it still makes my toes tingle."

Show Me, Lord

Several months prior to graduating from high school, Aaron began to look forward to heading off to college. His eagerness had nothing to do with leaving his family. Aaron loved his family -- even his little brother Casey and his sister Angela, one year his senior, who had decided to stay home for college.

Several months before Aaron headed off to college, he felt the Lord telling him that he was to go to college and then to seminary. Aaron was eager to get on with the life to which God had called him. Also, Aaron felt the Lord telling him that while he was in college he would meet his wife to be.

Four years later, Aaron still felt called to go to seminary, but the Lord had not yet revealed to him the woman he would spend the rest of his life with.

Aaron had dated a lot during those four years and each time Aaron met a new young woman he prayed and asked, "Lord, is this the one?"

But every time Aaron prayed that prayer, he felt no answer from God. After many dates and almost four years of college, Aaron no longer asked God. He still believed that God would let him know in His own way and in His time, but Aaron no longer prayed that prayer.

But with graduation coming soon, Aaron prayed again. "Lord, it's me again, Aaron. Lord, you know it's almost time for me to graduate and I don't feel that You've revealed to me the woman you have for me. Lord, if I misinterpreted your will, or if You're calling me to be patient just a little longer, please let me know so I can serve you better. Thank you, Lord, and please continue to lead me in the direction you want me to go. Amen."

After he prayed, Aaron went on to bed. He could not sleep. Aaron lay there continuing to praise God for leading him through almost four years of college and for giving him a ministry to other students and an occasional professor during his four years there.

Finally, Aaron went to sleep. He woke up in the middle of the night sweating profusely. Aaron did not know what to think. He checked his neck. He was not hot, nor did he feel sick, yet he was sweating.

Aaron headed to the bathroom to wipe off his brow. He returned to bed, but he could not go back to sleep. In a matter of minutes Aaron felt God speaking to him, not in an audible voice, but he felt God's presence nonetheless.

"Aaron, it's time," he felt God say. "Soon I will introduce you to the woman who will share your ministry."

Aaron's heart raced. He sat up in bed. After a few seconds and no other messages, Aaron got out of his bed and knelt beside it and prayed.

Aaron woke up the next morning refreshed and headed off to class. He met no new women at school that day. Still, Aaron trusted God and felt that He would soon show him the woman he would marry.

Aaron did not have to work that day. He headed to his apartment to do homework and study. As he was about to enter his apartment building, he heard someone call out.

"Excuse me."

"Were you talking to me?" Aaron asked as he saw a young woman approach.

Aaron's heart raced, much as it did the night before.

"Is your name Aaron?" the young woman asked.

"Yes. Do I know you?" Aaron replied.

"Not yet, and this may sound like the worst pick-up line you've ever heard, but for some reason I think I'm supposed to meet you."

Aaron began shaking and burst into tears.

"You feel it, too, don't you?" the young woman responded through tears of her own.

Aaron could only nod, but reached out to embrace the young woman.

A Dozen Roses

Marsha looked up as a delivery person entered the office carrying a dozen roses.

"Sure wish I'd get some roses sometime, but no way. The last time I received roses was when John took me to the prom, and I believe he only gave me one."

Marsha continued to look for a moment as Angela took the roses from the delivery man, and then Marsha returned to her work.

Marsha looked up again and noticed Angela standing in front of her grinning from ear to ear.

"Who did you get flowers from this time?" Marsha asked. Before Angela could answer, Marsha continued. "You'd better enjoy the single life, because after you get married no one sends you flowers anymore."

"You're wrong, Marsha."

"Well, we'll see. Do you know when was the last time anyone sent me flowers?"

"Uh huh," Angela answered, still grinning.

"Oh, I told you, did I?" Marsha replied.

"Nope, but I know when was the last time you got flowers."

"And when was that little Miss Know-It-All?"

"Today," Angela replied.

"Huh?" Marsha asked quizzically.

"These are for you, Marsha."

"You're kidding, of course."

"Nope. The card has your name on it."

"But who would send me flowers?"

"Your husband, I hope," Angela answered.

"I see you've never met my husband," Marsha replied.

"Don't you think we should find out before the roses wilt? Here. Where do you want me to put them? I have to get back to work."

Marsha cleared a spot in the middle of her desk and motioned for Angela to set down the flowers. Then Marsha waited until Angela went back to her desk and nervously reached for the card, opened it, and began to read.

"To Marsha, with all my love. Enjoy the roses and then put on this sparkling little number and meet me at Palatinos at 5:30. Then we'll put this hotel key to good use. Love, John."

"John. John who?" Marsha asked herself. "The only John I can think of is my husband. The closest he came to buying me flowers was when he brought home a package of flowers seeds."

Marsha read the card silently and realized the flowers must have come from her husband. Tears flowed from her eyes. She was overcome by what had happened. It took Marsha a few minutes before she asked herself, "What little number?"

"Hey, Angela!"

"What, Marsha?"

"There hasn't by any chance been another delivery today, has there?" Marsha asked.

Angela was ready to answer "no" when the door opened and in walked another delivery man with a large box.

"There has been now," Angela replied, causing Marsha to look up again.

As Marsha nervously opened the second box, the tears returned. Inside she found a black cocktail dress, a pair of shoes, a bottle of expensive looking perfume, and a key to a room at the fanciest hotel in the city. Because a friend of hers had stayed there one time, Marsha knew it was a key to the honeymoon suite.

It took a while before Marsha noticed Angela standing beside her. It had been a while since Marsha had seen a woman grin and cry at the same time. Marsha stood up and the two embraced. She was glad that they could share this moment without anyone else present.

In a few moments, Angela broke the silence.

"Well, Marsha. I guess he does still love you. You want me to tell Mr. Dorsey that you won't be in tomorrow?"

"You can tell Mr. Dorsey that I might not be back all week."

Reserved Seating

Lisa thought back to the day that turned her life around. She woke up that morning and found herself in an alley. She adjusted her underwear and tried to recall what had happened the night before. She could not remember.

Lisa sat in that alley and reflected on her recent life. She began to despise what she had become. Not yet twenty-two and already a drunk, or was that an alcoholic? She should never have listened to her friends.

"One won't hurt you."

"Drinking is cool."

"What do you think you are, a designated driver?"

As she sat in that alley despising herself, Lisa vowed that she would never again take a drink.

Lisa stood up. She straightened her clothes and combed her hair. When she was reasonably satisfied with how she looked, she tried to sneak out of the alley undetected.

As Lisa walked down the street, she noticed a church.

"Is this a coincidence, or is God trying to tell me something?" she asked herself.

Something caught Lisa's eye. Written below the name of the church, the time of the service, and the pastor's name, Lisa spotted something that read: "Reserved Seating. Please Hurry! We Have Only Two Reserved Seats Left. One Is For God. The Other Is For You."

The last time Lisa had felt any seat was reserved for her was when she was in high school. Lisa had captained her high school cheerleading team and the senior class elected her prom queen.

"From prom queen to alley litter," Lisa chastised herself. "My, how I've fallen! What day is this?"

She realized that it was Saturday. Touched by the words on that church sign, Lisa promised herself she would attend that church the next day.

Lisa awakened the next morning and wanted to turn over and go back to sleep, the way she usually did on Sunday morning. At least she usually did if she found herself waking up in her own bed. But that morning was different. That was the day Lisa planned to turn her life around.

She showered and dressed quickly, wanting to make sure she arrived at the church on time. Her excitement continued until she neared the church, and fear stepped in and slapped her in the face.

"What if someone at the church knows me? What if they don't really want me there?" she wondered.

Lisa almost turned around and went back home. She thought back to the morning before and gathered enough courage to rout out her fear.

Almost as soon as Lisa stepped inside the church people began to come up and introduce themselves.

"Hi, I'm Sue. Good to have you this morning?"

"Hi, I'm Allen, and this is my wife Tina."

"Don't they know who I am?" Lisa thought.

Lisa felt blessed that Sunday morning and returned the next week. A few weeks later she started attending a Sunday School class and joined the choir.

A year later, Lisa stood in the choir loft one Sunday morning. She remembered the morning she woke up in that alley. She thought of how much the church had meant to her.

Lisa looked over at Brian and Brian looked back and smiled.

"Wow! We've been dating six months. Brian is responsible for me volunteering at the mission. I wonder if I had never fallen if I would have met someone as special as Brian?"

Lisa looked at Rachel who stood next to Brian.

"Rachel's the one who gave me the courage to share my testimony. She's really become a special friend. I can't remember the last time I had a friend so special," Lisa continued to reflect.

"What if the alley where I woke up that morning was not near this church? What if I hadn't awakened that morning? Or what if I had decided to roll over and go back to sleep the next morning?" Lisa thought.

Lisa shuddered at the thought of how close she came to missing out on her new life with Brian, Rachel, and Jesus. As Lisa left the church that Sunday she paused in front of the sign. It was still there. There was still a reserved seat for God and whoever needed to find Him, whether he or she woke up in an alley or at home in bed.

Which Road

It seemed to Roger as if he had been on his journey for a long time. He knew where he wanted to go, but he had not gotten as far as he wanted or gotten there as quickly as he would have liked. The sky grew progressively darker and it grew more difficult for Roger to tell which route he should take.

Eventually, Roger came to a fork in the road, and he wondered which way he should go. He saw an abandoned service station and pulled in and mulled over his dilemma.

"Oh, God, why am I here? Which way do I go?" Roger pleaded.

A voice told him to take the road that turned to the right, but Roger felt the left one was the way to go, so he pulled away from the service station and headed down the left fork.

Not more than a minute later, panic crossed Roger's face. The "thump, thump, thump" told Roger his car had a flat tire. He pulled over to check. Roger got out of his car and saw that his left front tire was flat.

"Why me? I'm late. I'm lost. I'm helpless."

The flat tire, the darkened sky, and Roger's realization that he had no flashlight increased Roger's anxiety.

"What do I do now?"

Before Roger could come up with an answer, someone else shed some light on his situation. Roger used one hand to cover his eyes and waved frantically with the other one as a vehicle approached. While Roger's hands served a purpose, his feet remained firmly planted, and his position resembled that of a hypnotized deer.

As Roger's eyes adjusted, he realized that those headlights belonged to a tow truck.

The driver of the tow truck opened the door and jumped from the cab.

"Looks like you've got a little trouble."

"Looks like I have a lot of trouble, or at least I did until you showed up."

"What's the matter?"

"Flat tire."

"And no spare?" the tow truck driver asked.

"No, I've got a spare, but no flashlight and no x-ray vision."

"Well, I think I can take care of you."

"Everything seems to be going wrong for me today, and I'm late for an appointment," Roger said.

"Well, you just need to have faith that everything is going to turn out okay," the other driver responded.

In a few minutes the stranger had fixed the tire.

"Well, I think that should fix you up. I've got to go now. I need to help someone else who's taken the wrong road," the stranger said as he quickly hopped into the tow truck, turned the truck around, and headed off in the direction Roger was headed. The stranger left so quickly that Roger did not have time to thank him, pay him, or realize that the stranger made a reference that Roger had taken the wrong road.

"I wonder if he just happened along on his way to help someone else. At any rate, I'm a lucky man that he did," Roger thought, as he scratched his head and felt as if he had watched the Lone Ranger ride off into the distance.

Roger returned to his car and resumed his journey. Everything seemed much better until out of nowhere appeared a car speeding down the middle of the road. Roger jerked his car to the right, barely missing a collision with the oncoming car.

After taking a minute to regain his composure, Roger attempted to get back onto the road, but he soon found out that his car was stuck in the mud.

Roger got out and assessed his situation. "More   trouble," Roger muttered, as he realized he would be unable to get his car out of the mud without some assistance.

Roger began to think of the stranger's comments about "the wrong road" and had second thoughts about his choice of roads.

"Boy, I wish the guy in the tow truck would come back."

No sooner had Roger uttered these words when another set of headlights approached. They were coming from the wrong direction to be the man in the tow truck, but Roger thought whoever it was might still be someone who could help him.

The driver stopped and stepped down from his vehicle. Roger's mouth flew open.

"Bu...bu...but," is all Roger could mutter.

"I see you've gotten yourself in trouble again, my friend."

"How did you get here? I saw you head off in the other direction," Roger replied.

"Let's just say that sometimes I work in mysterious ways," replied the stranger who was already at work surmising the situation.

"But, no one passed me except that speeding car and that was definitely a car, not a tow truck."

Before Roger realized what was happening, the stranger had pulled Roger's car back onto the road.

"Well, I think that should take care of you."

"Thanks, again. I'm really sorry."

"You should have listened to me when I tried to tell you which road to take when you stopped back at my garage."

The stranger headed to his tow truck. Roger just stood there trying to figure what the stranger had meant. The only place he had stopped was the abandoned service station and he had not talked to anyone.

Roger looked up as the tow truck pulled off. Written on the side of the truck were the words: G. GRACE: WRONG ROAD WRECKER SERVICE.

Going To Jesus Celebration

Pastor Smallwood looked around the church and then turned to his oldest daughter Linda.

"Just look at all these people. The place is full. There's Percy White. I married him and Molly. And there's Jimmy Underwood. I baptized him. And over there's Betty Albertson. When that automobile accident took her parents away, I officiated at their 'Going To Jesus Celebration.'"

"Dad, forty-two years is a long time, you know."

"Still, it means a lot that they came. Of course I see some of them every Sunday, but some of these people came a long way to be here and I haven't seen them in years."

"Yeah, but Dad, they all love you and Mom."

"Yeah, I'm glad they all came for your mom today."

"They came for you, too, Dad."

Pastor Smallwood shifted uncomfortably while he waited for his associate pastor and a couple of close friends to speak. Then he reached over and grasped Linda's hand.

"It sure has been good having you and Gus here with me all these years. Your mom and I have enjoyed seeing the grandkids grow up in our church."

"It's been special to all of us, too, and we're not about to leave you now."

"You know your mom and I talked many times about this day. I just didn't expect her to go first. After all, a wife usually outlives her husband."

"I know this has to be tough on you, Dad."

"It is. Everything happened so suddenly. Just last Sunday your mom sat right next to Mrs. Florence, and now she's gone. I wonder which is tougher. Going quickly and not having a chance to say goodbye, or having time to say goodbye but enduring all that suffering."

"Well, at least Mom didn't suffer, Dad. We can be thankful for that much. And there's no doubt where Mom is now."

"You're right about that, Pumpkin."

"Why, Dad. You haven't called me Pumpkin since I was eight-years old."

"Well, that's because you said it embarrassed you."

"Well, it did then, but it's good to hear it again. Dad, are you sure you'll be all right?"

"As if I have a choice. I'm not about to commit suicide, you know."

"No, I mean you can stay with us for a while."

"I'll be honest with you. The thought of waking up and finding no one next to me, the thought of no one to talk to at breakfast, the thought of looking at your mother's empty rocker, they all scare me, but I have to face this. And besides, you're only five minutes away if I need you."

Linda leaned over and kissed her dad on the cheek and took his hand as they prepared to face her mother's Going To Jesus Celebration together.

Homeless No More

Everyone who lived or worked downtown knew Walt. That included the homeless and those who owned the downtown businesses.

All day long Walt rode by on his homemade four-wheel sled. He ran errands for everyone. Walt picked up breakfast or lunch for people, bought newspapers for them, and even took people's shoes to the repair shop. He served in any way he could.

Not only did Walt run errands for people, he shared his message that Jesus saves. Walt knew that, because Jesus saved him. Walt shared his testimony about the accident where he lost both of his legs. He told of his wife who left him because she did not want half a man.

Walt shared how he wanted to give up and how he had come to the streets he called home. Then Walt met Ol' Jedediah, who told Walt about Jesus and how much Jesus loved him.

Walt turned his life around that day. He still lived on the streets, slept in the park in the summer and in a boxed crate at the end of the alley in the winter, but Walt always helped anyone who needed help.

He kept very little of the money he earned running errands. He did not need it. He had no rent. He had no bills to pay. And just about every diner in town gave him leftovers to eat. What Walt did not give to the mission he gave to those who needed it. Walt gave to those in need who would not spend it on something to drink.

Only God knows how many people Walt turned away from drinking and to the Lord. Although everyone had to look down to see Walt, they all looked up to him, even the business owners. Everyone considered Walt one of a kind.

When Walt did not show up one day, Big Eddie went looking for him. Big Eddie found Walt in his crate at the end of the alley. Walt lay there with a smile on his face and a letter on his chest.

The letter read, "If you are reading this, it is because I'm homeless no more. I got a home today because Jesus went to prepare a place for me. I hope you will carry on my work and tell others about Jesus because he has a room for everyone."

They passed an ordinance that allowed Walt to be buried in the same park where he spent his summers. A plaque marked Walt's grave. The plaque read, "In honor of Walt, who was twice the man most of us are. Now, he is in heaven and he wants you to come and see him some day. If you don't know how to get there, ask anyone who knew Walt. He gave directions to all of them."

Christmas Joy

God had blessed Herbert. He was retired and had good enough health to enjoy his retirement. His wife Margaret had reasonably good health, as well. They lived close to their four children and nine grandchildren. Because God had truly blessed him, Herbert did his best to bless others.

One way Herbert chose to bless others was to dress up as Santa Claus at a local department store. While most malls only had a Santa, this department store had a Mrs. Santa, as well, as Margaret joined Herbert in his endeavor.

Many people said children were not like they used to be, but Herbert and Margaret found each child who sat on Herbert's lap to be as loving as their own children were when they were young.

One day, as the long lines waiting on Santa had diminished to nothing, Herbert noticed a small boy looking at him. The boy's jacket looked much too thin for that time of year, and his clothes looked like hand-me-downs.

"Come here," Herbert called out to the little boy.

The little boy merely shook his head "no."

"Come here and tell Santa what you want for Christmas this year," Herbert said, hoping to convince the little boy to come and sit on his lap.

"It won't do no good," the little boy said. "Mama says that we don't have enough money to pay you to bring us stuff."

Herbert looked over at Margaret and she nodded her approval. After fifty-two years of marriage, Herbert and Margaret could read each other's mind.

"You don't have to pay Santa to bring presents," Herbert answered. "Santa does that on his own."

"Don't go puttin' ideas in the boy's head," the boy's mother said after overhearing what Herbert had to say.

118

"We don't have no money for Christmas this year," she whispered to Herbert as she came closer.

"Don't worry about that," said Herbert. "Bring the child to me. Santa has his ways."

The boy's mother stood there trying to decide what to do.

"Trust me," Herbert said. "Santa has his ways."

The woman turned to her son. She hoped that she could believe the man inside the suit.

"It's okay, Jamal," the boy's mother said.

"Come on over here and sit on Santa's lap, Jamal, and tell Santa what you want for Christmas," Herbert said encouraging the boy to come to him.

Reluctantly, the boy came over and stood in front of Herbert and Herbert hoisted the boy onto his lap.

"So, Jamal, what do you want me to bring you this year?" Herbert asked.

"I don't know. I never thought, since mama said you weren't coming this year."

"Your mama thought I was too busy, but I'm never too busy. Now think and tell me what you want."

"You mean anything?" Jamal asked.

"Well, it would depend on whether or not I have it at the North Pole, but you can tell me what you want and when I get back I can see if I have it."

Jamal named a couple of things for himself and something he wanted for his mother and then hopped down.

"Whoa! Wait a minute little fellow. What's your hurry?"

"I'm not in no hurry. I just can't think of nothin' else."

"Are you sure that's all?"

"That's all I can think of," Jamal replied.

"Now, let me make sure I have your address right. Can you give it to me to make sure?"

Jamal looked at his mother who nodded her approval, and then he took out a card and handed it to Herbert to copy.

"Jamal, I forget. Do you have any brothers or sisters?" Herbert asked.

"Nope, no one except me and mama. Daddy ran away with some woman when I was a baby," Jamal shared matter of factly.

"Now, you remember to be a good boy, so I can come and see you."

Jamal's mother had no idea who was knocking quietly at her door late Christmas Eve night. Curious, she opened the door a crack to see a man in a Santa Claus' outfit.

Bursting into a big grin, she said, "You did come!"

"Of course, I came. I told Jamal I was coming, didn't I?" Herbert answered as he and Margaret unloaded a van load of gifts for Jamal and his mother.

"The packages are marked. Some are for Jamal and some are for you," Margaret told Jamal's mother.

"For me? No one has ever gotten me nothin'," Jamal's mother replied.

"Well, now they have. And by the way, here are some things for Christmas dinner. Look through the bag to see which ones need to go in the refrigerator," Margaret instructed Jamal's mother.

"Bless you," Jamal's mother said through her tears.

"God has blessed us, and may He bless you, too," Margaret replied.

"Merry Christmas," Herbert and Margaret whispered as they headed out the door.

"And a very Merry Christmas to you, too," Jamal's mother replied.

The Church Business Meeting

The phone call was not unexpected, but that did not keep it from being painful.

"Kathy, your mother has died," said the voice on the other end of the phone.

Kathy's father was dead and since Kathy was an only child, she would have to make the funeral arrangements.

"How am I ever going to get the money to go back home?" Kathy asked herself after hanging up. Even though it was only three hundred miles and she could stay at her parents' house, Kathy's mother's death came at a time when money was the tightest.

Kathy needed prayer. She called her church, shared her news with the secretary, and talked to her pastor.

"I'm so sorry, Kathy. Do you know when you and Jim are leaving?" her pastor asked.

"We've got to work some things out first, so we probably won't leave until tomorrow."

"Kathy, I want to stop by and pray with you and Jim after while, but first I want to get this on the prayer chain. Would that be okay?"

"That would we great! We should be here, but I'll call you if we have to go out for a few minutes."

Pastor Conklin knew that Jim had been laid off recently and so did everyone in their church. Pastor Conklin knew others in the church would want to do whatever they could for Kathy and Jim.

A couple hours later Jim and Kathy's doorbell rang.

"Hi, Joe. It's so good of you to stop by," Kathy said as she opened the door to let her pastor in.

"Kathy, everyone knows how tough things are for you and Jim right now. Some of the folks at church put in some money to help you with the trip. There should be enough for food, gas, and to stay at a motel if you decide you don't want to stay at your mother's place."

"I don't know what to say, Jim."

"Kathy, you know our church has always tried to be like Christ, both inside and outside the doors of the church. Remember when Henry Blackwell broke his leg and couldn't work on the farm? Remember how everyone pitched in and helped out?"

"I sure do. That's one of the reasons Jim and I chose this church."

"Kathy, I don't mean to meddle, but do you have enough to take care of the funeral?"

"Mom learned about funeral expenses when Dad died, and she didn't want to be a burden on Jim and me. She made her funeral arrangements and paid for everything. There was just enough, but enough."

Just after daylight the next day Kathy and Jim packed the car and left for her childhood home. A few hours later Kathy arrived and headed to the funeral home to set the times for visitation and the service. Visitation was set for the next afternoon and evening with the funeral the following morning.

Jim made Kathy take something to help her sleep that night. It did its job. Visitation began at 3:00 p.m. By five o'clock, only one person had stopped by, a hospital nurse who had helped take care of Kathy's mother. It had been years since Kathy had lived in her hometown. Kathy's mother had outlived all of her friends, so Kathy was not expecting a large turnout at the funeral home.

Still, the lack of visitors was starting to take its toll on Kathy when in came a familiar face.

"Why, Joe! I sure didn't expect to see you here!"

"Why, where did you expect me to be, Kathy?"

"Why, at the church business meeting, of course."

"Well, I am at the church business meeting, Kathy. After all, part of the business of the pastor is meeting the needs of those in the congregation."

Kathy was still sad about her mother's passing, but when she went to bed that night she was most thankful for the man in the guest room of her mother's house. He was indeed a friend.

What A Treat

The people in Greg's church were divided. Some of them looked at Halloween as an innocent time where children went from door-to-door in their neighborhood having fun and coming home with enough candy to last a week. Others called it "The Night Of The Devil."

To Greg, Halloween had a different meaning. Each Halloween he thought back to the last time he went trick-or-treating. He almost did not go. After all, he had turned twelve. Some of his friends thought they were too big to go trick-or-treating. Finally, Greg decided he would go. He was glad he went. If he had not gone, he probably would not have become a pastor.

Greg went home and dumped out his big bag full of goodies. He was eager to see if he had gotten any of his favorites candies. Greg always gave his little brother the ones he did not want, because his little brother would eat anything.

Greg was disappointed that the biggest treat of all was not candy. Someone had given him a Bible. Who would do something like that? Greg took it to his room. He was not sure what he would do with it. He was sure if he threw it away God would punish him.

The Bible sat on Greg's table for several weeks. On Christmas Eve, he noticed it lying there and remembered that it contained the story of Jesus' birth. Greg decided to look for the story. It took him a while, but he found it.

Surprisingly, the Christmas Story sounded kind of cool, so Greg decided to read more. He checked out many different books of his Bible, but some of them did not seem as interesting as others.

One day Greg told one of his friends that he had been reading the Bible. He found out that his friend attended church. Greg began to think. Maybe going to church could be cool, too.

Greg decided to go home and ask his mother if they could go to church. His mother did not like the idea. Then Greg decided to ask his father, but he got the same answer.

Finally, Greg came up with an idea that might work. He decided to have his little brother ask their mother about going to church. Greg's mother always did everything his little brother wanted to do.

Greg's brother did not want to ask. Greg bribed his brother with two candy bars. Greg found out that his mother could say "no" to his little brother, too.

Greg wanted to go to church, so he persisted. Finally, a few months later, his parents relented. They were not against going to church. They were in favor of sleeping late.

Soon Greg became involved in the youth group. He became close friends with his youth pastor, and he began to think about how some day he might want to help some boy like his youth pastor had helped him.

Years passed, youth group ended and college began. Greg's desire for the ministry increased. Greg finished college and enrolled in seminary. While attending seminary, he got a job as a youth pastor. After he graduated, he became the pastor of a church.

Since someone cared enough to give Greg a Bible for Halloween, Greg planned to be home on Halloween handing out Bibles to each child who stopped by. After all, some day a church might need a new pastor.

Fisher Of Humans

Nathan loved to eat out. He used that time to put into practice his unique ministry. While Nathan ate, he watched people. Sometimes, if a packed restaurant caused him to wait for a table, Nathan struck up a conversation with some of the others who waited.

"Have you eaten here before?" Nathan asked on many occasions, whether he had eaten at that particular restaurant or not. This led to more conversation, which Nathan used as he decided his project for the evening.

Almost every night Nathan found a project. Nathan scanned the restaurant and decided who it would be. To determine the recipient of his act of kindness, Nathan asked himself who looked like they needed help in one way or another, or who had made his wait a little more pleasant.

If the restaurant seated him immediately, Nathan found a reason to leave his table, such as a trip to the restroom. On his way he would stop and talk with a customer.

"You sure have a pretty baby. Is it a boy or a girl?" Nathan would ask a young couple in order to initiate a conversation.

"Excuse me, but I see you ordered the Veal Scaloppini. I'm thinking about ordering it, too. Is it any good?" Nathan would ask.

Nathan did not care whether they liked their entree or not. He wanted an excuse to talk to someone. Many times Nathan watched people as they ate. When Nathan decided who would receive a free meal from him, he caught their server's attention.

"Excuse me, but aren't you waiting on that table over there?"

"Yes sir, I am."

"Well, I want to pick up their tab. Just bring it to me when they finish."

Nathan delighted in seeing his recipients faces when their server told them the good news. Many times Nathan's recipients stopped by and thanked him before they left. On those occasions Nathan asked them if they had ordered dessert. If they said "no," Nathan invited them to stay and enjoy dessert with him.

After taking a few minutes to get to know them better, Nathan asked a question.

"Why do you think more people don't attend church?"

After they answered his question, Nathan asked whether or not they attended church. If they said "yes", he asked what they liked about their church.

If they said "no," Nathan began to tell them why he liked his church. Nathan shared the message of Jesus Christ with many people he met.

Not everyone Nathan talked to accepted Christ, and some of his recipients already had a relationship with Him. Nathan did lead some of them to Christ and he stayed in regular contact with each one of them.

If Nathan left the restaurant before those who received a free meal because of him, he handed the waiter a note to give to the recipients. The note explained his ministry.

He said if they had questions, wanted to know more about Jesus, or were looking for a church, they could contact him. The note contained his address, phone number, and e-mail address. Many contacted Nathan. Some contacted Nathan to thank him for his generosity. Sometimes this led to a new life for someone.

Not only did Nathan share his generosity with the restaurant's customers, but with the servers as well. Instead of a tip, Nathan left a note with his address. He told each server that he had a $25.00 tip for them and told them they could stop by and pick it up.

Some did stop by, but many did not. When a server came to Nathan's home, he gave them a choice. They could either have $25 on the spot, or they could come back at a specific time the next day and he would double the tip to $50.

Some opted for the bird in the hand. Others came back the next day. When they returned, Nathan told them if they would return again the next day, he would double the tip again to $100. Nathan promised them, without fail, he would give them $100 the next day. There would be no more trips.

Some thought two trips were enough, but some decided to test him one more time and make a third trip. When someone showed up for the third time, Nathan invited him or her in and told them to have a seat while he went and got the money.

As Nathan handed the money to the server, he said, "Now you probably think that I am giving you a lot of money. I'm really not, and it'll probably be gone soon, but let me tell you about something that can last you a lot longer than this $100."

Nathan began to share the Gospel of Jesus Christ. While a few made an excuse that they had somewhere else they had to be, most stayed and listened, since Nathan had given them $100.

Nathan had no idea how many his ministry had led to Christ, but he knew there were some. One was a young woman who contacted him many years later. She came back to pick up the $100, but did not want to hear what he had to say.

The young woman never thought of Nathan again until one day when everything went wrong, and she did not have enough money to pay her bills. At that moment she prayed and asked God for another customer like Nathan. Realizing she had prayed, she cried and prayed again, and then looked in her purse to find the address of the man who might be able to help her find the right direction.

Billy's Christmas Present

It was Christmas Eve. Billy's mother had decorated for Christmas, but to six-year-old Billy it did not seem like Christmas.

Not only were there no presents under the tree, but this was Billy's first Christmas without his dad. He tried to remember that his dad had gone to be with Jesus, but that did not always comfort Billy.

His mother tried to comfort him, but she was lonely and hurting, too; however, she tried not to show it in front of Billy.

Billy's mother tried to explain to him that Santa would not be coming. Billy did not understand.

Billy's mother tucked him in bed, and he tried to go to sleep. The moisture on Billy's pillow showed that he was struggling with his predicament.

When Billy awoke the next morning, he bounded from his bed hoping that Santa had come anyway. When Billy reached the living room, he came to an abrupt halt. Billy stared at the emptiness below the tree.

Billy's mother came up behind him and put her hand on his shoulder. He turned around and noticed her tears.

"I'm sorry, Billy," she said as she gave him a big hug.

"It wasn't you fault, Mom. Santa was the one who didn't come."

"Come here, Billy. Let's sit down and I'll read you the story about Jesus' birth."

Billy had become used to hearing the story of Jesus' birth on Christmas morning, but it had always been his dad who had read it. Billy listened as his mother read the story to him.

"Come on, soldier. I'm going to fix you a special breakfast," she said after they had read and discussed the story.

The thought of breakfast made Billy perk up and momentarily forget about the lack of presents. Billy wanted presents, but he wanted his dad more than anything.

As Billy and his mother tried to decide what to do after breakfast, they heard a knock at the door. They wondered who was knocking. Billy was pretty sure Santa never came that late.

Billy ran to the door. He got to the door and opened it. A young man stood at the door. Billy did not recognize him.

"Are you Billy?" the stranger asked.

"Uh, yeah," Billy answered. "How do you know my name?"

Billy failed to notice that the young man carried a present under his arm, a present wrapped in shiny red paper.

When Billy's mother got to the door, the stranger introduced himself. "Hi, I'm Josh. I'm Billy's Big Brother. I just found out who my Little Brother was last night and almost didn't have time to get him a present. Here, Billy. This is for you."

"Come in, Josh. I'm Laura, Billy's mother. Let me take your hat and coat."

Billy was excited. When he saw nothing under the tree, he figured he was not getting anything for Christmas. Billy tore through the paper and ripped open the box. Inside he found a football.

"A football! Gee, thanks!" Billy shouted.

"You're welcome, Billy. Do you like it?"

"Like it? It's awesome! My old one got run over by a car. Wait until Jason hears about this."

"Billy, do you know what a Big Brother is?" Josh asked.

"You mean like B.J.'s big brother?"

"No, not that kind. There's an organization called Big Brothers where guys volunteer to spend time with boys who don't have a father. I'll be your Big Brother."

"You mean you'll come over sometimes and spend time with me and do things together?"

"That's right, Billy."

"Boy, wait until I tell Jason that I got a Big Brother for Christmas. Hey, Josh. Could we go outside and toss the ball around?"

Sure, if it's okay with your mom."

"It's okay with me, Billy, but you have to dress warm."

"Aw, Mom. It's not that cold. Anyway, it's hard to throw the ball with a lot of stuff on."

Billy and Josh played for an hour. Billy could have played longer. When he went to bed that night Billy thought about his new friend and his football. It seemed that Santa came after all, or was it Jesus?

The Long Walk

Jim's knees buckled every few feet. He grasped his wife's hand, and the two of them began the longest walk of their lives.

Only the day before, Jim looked down at his lifeless, blood-stained daughter, lying crumpled in the front seat of her car.

If only Jim had insisted that he lead. It would have been him lying there instead of his daughter, and wasn't a father supposed to die before his daughter?

But Kailey insisted that she lead the way. Because she had, the out-of-control oncoming car slammed into her car head-on.

Kailey died instantly. Jim did not even get a chance to tell her goodbye, even though he followed her in his car.

As Jim and Carol looked down at Kailey's casket, they did their best to hold back the tears. They looked down at her lifeless body. She looked at peace. She was wearing the lilac dress she had planned to wear to her graduation.

Jim and Carol did their best to control their emotions. They had to hold up for their other children and face all the family and friends who would be coming soon.

Jim and Carol wanted to be an example for Kailey's friends. Kailey's friends would want to know why this had to happen to someone so young and full of life who had so much love for God and others.

Jim wanted to convey to Kailey's friends that they needed to turn to God. Jim and Carol credited the presence of the Holy Spirit and the love of their friends for helping them get through their trying time.

Jim had thought many times of a walk when he thought of Kailey, but it was not this type of walk that he had in mind. Jim thought of a walk down the aisle of a church, but that would never happen. Kailey was gone. There would not be any more happy events to look forward to, only happy memories.

Kailey would not be rushing in to show off an engagement ring. Jim and Kailey would not walk down the aisle together. There would be no wedding reception and no father-daughter dance. There would be no grandchildren. There would only be memories of first words, first steps, first days at school, and a first driving lesson.

Jim turned to Carol and embraced her, but only momentarily because they heard the footsteps of their other two children who were making the longest walk of their young lives.

Earth Angel

Angel awakened. Her throbbing headache reminded her that she was suffering from another hangover. When she became aware of her surroundings, she realized she was in her car. It was not the first morning Angel woke up and found herself in such a predicament.

Angel sat up to see where she was. When she saw that she was parked in front of a church, she fought the urge to dive back to the seat. It was Sunday morning and people were walking past her car and into the church.

Angel felt a voice telling her that she, too, was to go to this church. She tried to resist, but the voice seemed insistent. Angel found herself agreeing with this voice. She adjusted the mirror and began to comb her hair and reapply her make-up without thinking about her rumpled clothes and drunken odor that surely would have changed her mind.

As she opened the door and got out, Angel noticed a man asleep in the back seat of her car. He did not look familiar. She could not remember anything about the night before, and she shuttered when she tried to figure out how he came to be there.

Angel decided not to awaken the sleeping stranger and quietly closed the door and began her difficult climb up the church steps.

Angel slid into the back pew. Luckily, the congregation was singing, so no one realized that she was there. This was the first time Angel had been inside a church in some time. She soon found herself becoming more involved in the service than she was in wondering if anyone was looking at her.

The pastor's sermon was like nothing she had experienced in a long time. Not only did she need to hear his words, but she became engrossed in them.

Before she knew it, the pastor gave an altar call. Angel wanted to go forward but did not want to draw attention to herself. Angel felt someone give her a nudge and before she knew it she had stepped into the aisle.

Angel felt this someone pushing her forward toward the front of the church. Someone was insistent that she go forward. She glanced over her shoulder, but saw no one.

Angel continued down the aisle to the altar and knelt down and began to pray. As she did so, tears streamed down her cheeks. The pastor came over and knelt beside her. He whispered to Angel and she answered him. They continued to talk, and she began to share her life story with him.

The pastor prayed for Angel, and they shared a few more words before standing. As they stood up, the pastor clasped his hands around Angel's and shared a few more words of encouragement. Then he asked Angel if she would be willing to remain at the altar while he gave the benediction.

Angel had forgotten about the other people. She was surprised when she turned around and noticed that the church was still full. No one had left and some of the people had shed tears as well.

After the pastor gave the benediction, many people came up to greet Angel instead of turning to talk to friends or hurrying out of the church. As people hugged Angel, her tears started to flow again.

"We would like for you to come home with us for Sunday dinner," one lady said.

"You don't understand. I've been drinking." Angel replied.

"I know that, and the invitation is still good," the lady responded.

Angel's confession reminded her of her circumstances an hour before. She still had no idea who the man was in the back seat of her car, but she knew the one who drove her there must have been Jesus.

God's Grace

Bob lost his job and soon found out that there were no other jobs in his field in the small town where he lived. When he heard of another town where there was a possibility of a job, Bob loaded up his family and their few possessions and headed off in pursuit of that job. Bob arrived too late. There had been a job available, but it had been filled.

Heartbroken, Bob did not know what to do next, so he did what he always did when he did not seem to have an answer. He prayed to the One who has all the answers.

Bob felt like God was telling him to take the road leading west out of town. He shared this revelation with Marsha, who was supportive, just as she had always been. Bob always remembered to thank God for Marsha and the children. They were always a blessing, and many times they seemed to be his only blessing.

Bob and his family got an early start the next morning. They managed to drive a couple hundred miles before lunch. They arrived at a town that looked large enough to have some job opportunities. Bob stopped to buy a newspaper, hoping to find that elusive job.

After lunch, a much needed nap for all, and scouring the newspaper to no avail, Bob felt defeat once more. Just as he was about to toss the newspaper, he noticed an ad for a church a few miles up the road.

"Was this a sign from God?" Bob wondered.

No matter how bad things got for Bob, he never missed church. Bob decided that he, Marsha, and the children would attend that church the next day. It was getting quite late. Bob pulled over at a roadside park so Marsha could fix some sandwiches and they could get some much needed sleep.

They were all quite tired after a couple of days of traveling, and that became quite obvious when they overslept the next morning. When they awoke, Bob realized that there was no way they would be able to get to that church in time for the service. That disappointed him, but then Bob looked up and saw a small church nestled in the trees nearby. He decided to drive over and check it out.

As Bob drove up, he heard the congregation burst into song. He rushed everyone out of the car and into the church. As they entered the church, people turned around. Bob was sure everyone was wondering who were these people who looked like they had spent the night in their car.

Bob's apprehension was short-lived. People began to smile and nod at Bob's family. A couple of them came up and handed Bob and Marsha their song books, which were opened to the right page.

Bob was moved by the service. When the service ended many people came up and introduced themselves.

"Hi, I'm Ted. You're not from around here, are you?"

"No, we're from out-of-town. We were just passing through and saw your church," Bob replied.

"Why don't you and your family come over to our house for dinner. We have plenty and we'd really enjoy the company?" Ted asked.

"Are you sure you have food to spare. There are four of us," Bob replied.

"I'm sure. Alice always fixes enough for an army," Ted said exaggerating a little.

"Well, to be honest with you, I am getting tired of eating Marsha's sandwiches. Oh, I didn't mean it that way," Bob said.

"That's okay, and just in case you're wondering, we aren't having sandwiches," Ted responded.

After dinner, Ted and Alice wished Bob and Marsha good luck, and gave them some food to take with them.

Bob headed down the road. He had gone only two or three miles when steam started seeping up from under the hood. Bob got out and opened his hood to see what was wrong. He was still looking under the hood and trying to figure out what to do when a car came along and stopped.

When the guy got out, Bob recognized him as one of the other men they met at church that morning.

"Hello again! It looks like you've got a little trouble. Do you have any idea what's wrong?" the man asked.

"Not yet. I just got the hood up," Bob replied.

"Well, let me take a look. I own a garage just up the road. By the way, my name's Ray."

"I'm Bob. That's my wife Marsha, and the kids Tommy and Cindy."

Ray looked under the hood to see what was wrong.

"I'm sorry, but it looks like you need a tow. Want me to tow it in for you and take a look?"

"If that's what it takes, let's do it if you have the time," Bob responded, grateful for any help he could get.

"I'll be back with my wrecker in a jiffy."

In a few minutes Ray returned. He hooked up Bob's car to the wrecker, and they headed down the road.

While Ray was looking at the car to see what was wrong with it, he and Bob talked.

"What brought you to our neck of the woods?" Ray asked.

"Well, I just lost my job and I couldn't find anything else back home," Bob replied.

Bob went on to tell Ray about the type of work he did and was grateful that he did.

"Really! I have a friend a couple hours up the road who might be able to use you. I'll give him a call after we see what's wrong with your car," Ray said.

"Boy, that would be great!" Bob replied, excited about the possibility of a break.

By the time the car was fixed it was getting quite late.

"Bob, we've got a couple of spare bedrooms upstairs. Why don't you spend the night with us, and then, in the morning I can call my friend about the job?"

"Well, I'll tell you, Ray. After a couple of nights in the car a bed sounds really good right now."

When Bob woke up the next morning Ray had good news.

"I made a call and you have an interview tomorrow morning, my friend."

Bob was so moved he could not speak. Maybe his luck was about to change. Bob and his family showered, ate breakfast, and packed the car.

"Ray, how much do I owe you?"

"Well, Bob, you don't me anything. You owe someone else," Ray replied.

"I don't understand what you mean," Bob said, looking befuddled.

"Bob, I don't want any money for the work I did. I just want you to do a favor for the next person you see who could use your help. Does that sound fair enough?"

"It sounds fair enough to me, but are you sure?" Bob asked.

"I'm very sure! Now get out of here and go get that job!"

Not only did Bob get the job, but it paid more than the job he had lost.

A few days later, one of the other employees asked Bob how he got the job. Bob proceeded to tell his co-worker the story.

"You have a funny look on your face. What's it all about?" Bob asked.

"Bob, I've never been to the church God led you to, but on the way back from vacation one year I did go to the church you planned to attend."

"And?" Bob asked.

"Well, let's just say that I think you made the right choice."

"I assume you didn't like the other church," Bob surmised.

"I don't like to talk about others, but I wasn't impressed. The pastor seemed like he was just biding his time until retirement and only one family spoke to us and that was to let us know we were sitting in their pew."

"I think maybe God helped us oversleep that Sunday morning," Bob said.

A few weeks later, Bob was driving and spotted a car that was stopped by the side of the road. A man was standing beside the car. Bob thought about stopping, but he noticed the man had long hair and was not clean shaven.

As he was about to drive on, Bob remembered Ray's words.

"Bob, I don't want any money for the work I did. I just want you to do a favor for the next person you see who could use your help. Does that sound fair enough?"

Bob pulled over to see how he could help the young man. After they had spoken for a couple of minutes, the young man asked Bob a question.

"Why did you stop when so many others just drove on?" he asked Bob.

Bob then proceeded to tell the young man his story. After Bob had finished, the young man decided to share something with him.

"I've been here over two hours. The only man who stopped told me he was in a hurry and could not help me, but gave me something to read which told about Jesus, and told me that he would pray for me," the young man said.

"After that man left I cried out to Jesus and told him that if he was really there to prove it by sending someone to help me. I guess you're that someone," the young man said.

Bob began to tell the young man more about Jesus, and the man ended up asking Jesus into his life. Bob thought about the job he lost and the job he just missed getting. He thought of the time his family overslept and did not get to go to the church he had planned to attend. He thought of the family who fed his family and the man who fixed his car and gave him shelter. As Bob recalled these moments, he wondered, "If just one of these things had not happened to me, would anyone have ever shared the good news of Jesus Christ with this young man?

Family Reunion

"Yes?" the elderly woman said as she answered the door.

"I'm here to see about the room," the young lady replied.

"It's $425 a month and that includes meals and your own full bath. I don't allow loud music or a TV blaring late at night. Are you still interested?"

"Yes, ma'am, I sure am."

"My name's Mrs. Harrison, but everyone calls me Mrs. H."

"I'm K.D. Harmon, Mrs. H."

"Well, come along K.D. and I'll show you the room. You don't mind an upstairs room, do you?"

"Upstairs is fine. My new friend tried to get me to room with her, but I wanted to be close to campus since I don't have a car."

"This is definitely close to campus. Well, here's the room. What do you think?"

"It looks great to me. I'll take it. Can I move in today?"

"You sure can. Now go get your stuff and I'll fix us some lunch."

Like most college freshmen, K.D. had worried about finding a good place to stay. After living with Mrs. H. for a few days, K.D. figured God must have sent her this nice room, because Mrs. H. spoiled her.

Every morning when K.D. got up Mrs. H. would have breakfast ready. Every night Mrs. H. served supper just at the moment K.D. needed a break from her studies.

One morning K.D. got up a little early and came in just as Mrs. H. finished reading her Bible.

"That's some good reading you've got there, Mrs. H."

"The best there is," Mrs. H. replied.

"What did you read today?"

"The 23rd Psalm."

"Leading you beside those still waters, huh?"

"Yes, and restoring my soul."

K.D. enjoyed talking about the Bible with Mrs. H. Each day K.D. made it a point to ask Mrs. H. what she had read that morning. This led to a discussion around the breakfast table. One day brought them more than either of them expected.

"What did you read this morning, Mrs. H.?"

"Luke Chapter 15," Mrs. H. replied.

"All the lost stuff. A coin, a sheep, and a pig-feeding son."

"W-w-what was that you said?" Mrs. H. asked.

"I said, 'All the lost stuff. A coin, a sheep, and a pig-feeding son,'" K.D. repeated.

Mrs. H. looked visibly shaken.

"W-w-why did you say 'a pig-feeding son?'" Mrs. H. asked.

"Oh, that's the way my mom said my grandmother said it. I guess it just stuck with me. Are you okay, Mrs. H.?"

"I...I'm fine. Tell me, K.D. What does the K and the D stand for?"

"It's Kimberly Dawn, Mrs. H. My real mother named me that."

"Y-y-your real mother?"

"Yeah, you see, I'm adopted. The Harmons adopted me when my mother died."

"S-s-so Harmon wasn't the name you were born with?"

"No, it was Lancaster. My father died when I was a baby and my mother died in a car wreck a few years later. The only other relative I had was my grandmother. The authorities tried to find her, but they couldn't. One reason I chose this college is because my grandmother lived here at one time. Her name was...."

"Smithfield," Mrs. H. said, as she finished K.D.'s sentence.

"You're crying Mrs. H. Did you know my grandmother?"

"Come here, baby. You don't know how hard I've tried to find you. I've outlived two husbands. Mr. Harrison was the second one. Oh, baby! Thank you, Jesus, for bringing my baby back to me."

142

In Time For Sunday Morning

It was Saturday morning. Pastor Johnson sat in his study preparing the next day's sermon. He had been there for almost an hour, but the computer monitor was filled with nothing but a white screen. No words came to him.

It was not the first time he had been in that situation. Fifty sermons each year had a draining effect on the creative juices, and it had been twenty-three weeks since his vacation.

Pastor Johnson usually prepared his sermon early in the week. At least he did in those weeks when God spoke to him early in the week and he had time to prepare it.

Pastor Johnson pastored an elderly congregation. Many of them were not in good health. Pastor Johnson found himself preaching too many funerals and not performing enough weddings.

Mr. Zander had been in poor health for several months. Pastor Johnson preached Mr. Zander's funeral on Friday, after spending most of Thursday with Mrs. Zander. The Zanders were a saintly couple.

Pastor Johnson sat there a while longer, but no words came to him. About eleven o'clock, he got up, left the house, and walked next door to the church. The biting wind hit him in the face and the snow melted as it hit his cheeks. It was a typical late January day.

He pushed open the creaking door of the old church. He never locked it. Someone might want to come in and pray or feel the presence of God, and he wanted to make the church available to anyone anytime they felt the need.

Pastor Johnson rustled over to the stove and lit it. In a few minutes his body became nice and toasty. He walked across the wooden floor until he came to the altar. He knelt down to pray.

Pastor Johnson did not know how long he prayed. When he got up, his wife stood holding a couple of sandwiches and a thermos of coffee.

"I thought you might be able to use something to eat," Mrs. Johnson said.

"You always seem to know what I need," her husband replied.

"It comes with experience. Now give me a hug and I'll get out of your way," his wife responded.

Pastor Johnson tried to think as he ate, but still the words did not come. He walked over to the window. He hoped to see something which would inspire him. The snow was quite heavy, but the words were still sparse.

He walked over and sat in a pew. He stared at the cross, but still no words came. He took off his shoes and laid down in the pew. Finally, something had an effect on him. He awoke a few minutes later, but still without words. He went and stood in the pulpit. He opened his Bible and read, but after much time there, it, too, was to no avail.

The skies began to darken and so did his spirit. God had never taken this long to give him a sermon. He wondered if God was trying to teach him a lesson.

Pastor Johnson went to the window and looked at the light in the window at the parsonage. He wondered what his wife and kids were doing. He wished he was there to find out, but the sermon would have to come first.

He walked across the hardwood floor to the other side of the church and looked out the window. He saw many lights in the distance. No one would venture out on a such a night.

Pastor Johnson spotted a light in Mrs. Zander's home. He wondered how she was doing. She seemed to be fine when he called on her early that morning.

He looked across the road from her home to the Sanders home. He thought back to when he first moved to the community. At first, he thought that the Zanders and the Sanders were the same family. He figured that some people pronounced the name one way, while others did it another. That is until both families called on his family a few days later to welcome him and his family to their new home.

After standing there a few moments, Pastor Johnson went back to sit down. He closed his eyes and tried to think, but still no words came to him. He kept his eyes closed until he heard the door creak open. He looked up to see Mrs. Zander. Snow covered her wool coat.

"Why, Mrs. Zander? What brings you out on a night like this?"

"You do, pastor. I suspect you haven't finished your sermon, and I thought a hearty bowl of homemade soup might help," she replied.

"Why bless you, Mrs. Zander. It sounds just like what I need. God only knows how many times you've been a blessing."

Pastor Johnson enjoyed his visit with Mrs. Zander so much that he forgot all about the sermon he had to write.

"Why, pastor! Look at what time it is! Now eat your soup before it gets cold," Mrs. Zander coaxed. "I'm going to stay right here until you finish."

"You don't need to tell me again, Mrs. Zander. Don't tell my wife, but your soup is the best I've ever had."

After Pastor Johnson finished his soup, Mrs. Zander rose as if to leave.

"I guess I'd better go now, pastor. It's almost my bed time."

"I'll walk you home, Mrs. Zander." Off they went arm in arm. In a few minutes the pastor arrived back at his study and immediately began to write the sermon God gave him for the next morning.

Why Me, Lord?

The day had become too much for Whitney. She had been married only two weeks. She began the day by dropping off her husband at the airport. Whitney had never spent a night alone, and she was not looking forward to the first time.

Whitney scoffed down a drive-thru breakfast in order to get to work on time. She pulled out into traffic and headed to work. A man in the next lane cut in front of her without looking. His inattentive driving caused Whitney to hit her brakes and spill the last bit of her orange juice on her new outfit.

"Jerk!" Whitney hollered. Whitney had learned a lot from all those years of riding with her dad.

As she arrived at work, Whitney quickly got out of her car and headed inside. She was two minutes late.

"Miss Templeton, you are late this morning. That is not a good way to impress your new boss," Mr. Andrews hollered as he looked at his watch.

"I'm sorry, Mr. Andrews. I'll never let it happen again," Whitney uttered, while under her breath she said, "It's Mrs. Templeton, and don't ever forget that."

Whitney was not sure whether the big boss had gotten on Mr. Andrews or if his team had lost the night before. She only knew that his attitude was not what she needed on the day she sent off her one true love to another state for a week's training for his new job. Whitney reminded herself that he would only be gone one week.

Mr. Andrews was not the only one who was in a bad mood that day. Mrs. Thornapple must have been rooting for the same team as Mr. Andrews.

Whitney looked at her watch. Only 9:47.

"9:47," Whitney thought. "I'm ready to go home and it isn't even lunch time."

Whitney planned to pick up the dry cleaning on her lunch hour, only on this particular day it seemed that everyone else picked the same fast food restaurant she did. Whitney decided to wait and pick it up after work, just in case Mr. Andrews was on the warpath when she returned from lunch.

Whitney counted the minutes until 5:00. Around 3:45 Mr. Andrews came in.

"Miss Templeton, I need for you to stay a little late tonight. I have something that must be in the morning mail. I hope you don't mind. After all, I heard your husband has gone away."

Mr. Andrews's words stuck in Whitney's throat.

"Uh, sure, Mr. Andrews," was all she could reply.

Whitney finished work and hurried to the dry cleaners. She knew she had nothing to wear to work the next day. She arrived at the dry cleaners just as the clerk turned the sign to "Closed".

Whitney pounded on the door. "Please let me in! I have to have my clothes, so I'll have something to wear to work tomorrow," Whitney pleaded, but to no avail.

"I'm sorry, but you should have thought of that earlier. We have lives, too, you know," said the nasal voice from the other side of the glass.

Dejectedly, Whitney turned away. She planned to look for a new dry cleaners the next day.

When she was most of the way home, adversity hit Whitney again.

"Thump, thump, thump," came the sound which sounded like the right rear tire.

Whitney pulled over and began to bawl.

"Why me, Lord?" Whitney cried out as she rested her head on the steering wheel, fairly sure she knew how Job and Wile E. Coyote must have felt.

Whitney was interrupted a couple minutes later when she heard a knock on her window. She looked up to see a man with a pleasant smile, and she rolled down the window a bit.

"Is something wrong, Miss?" the stranger asked.

"It would be quicker if I told you what's right," Whitney replied.

"Maybe you could start with why you've pulled over," the stranger said.

"I think I've got a flat tire. To be honest, I haven't gotten out to check yet. I think it's the right rear tire. Would you mind checking it for me?"

"Be glad to. Just a second, Miss."

In a few seconds the man returned.

"You're right, Miss. Would you like for me to change it?"

"If you don't mind. That would be great."

The stranger stood there looking at Whitney.

"Is something wrong? Do I need to pay you first?"

"You don't need to pay me at all, but you do need to pop your trunk so I can get out your spare. You do have a spare, don't you?"

"Oh, yeah. Sorry," Whitney said as she reached down and pushed the button that opened her trunk.

In a few minutes the man had finished and Whitney headed on her way. She drove home and turned down her street. Whitney noticed several police cars, and they were in front of her house. She got out of the car and ran toward her house.

"I'm sorry, ma'am, but I can't let you through," an officer said as he stepped between Whitney and the house.

"But I live there, officer! That's my house!"

"Well, ma'am, if that's your house, you are one lucky lady."

"Why's that, officer?" Whitney asked.

"Ma'am, we just captured a burglar coming out of your house. One of the neighbors saw him jimmy a back window and climb through it and she called us. We were already here and ready for him when he came out. Ma'am, he came out shooting. If you'd come home any sooner, he might have shot you."

Stunned by the officers words, Whitney thought to herself. "Why me, Lord? Why did you decide to save me today?"

Arthur's Gift

If someone had driven by and looked at Arthur's house that day, they would have thought "there lives the American success story," and by the world's standards Arthur was a success.

He lived in a luxurious mansion at the end of a long tree-lined driveway and behind the house was a swimming pool, tennis courts and a garage housing his eight automobiles. He had acquired enough wealth that he would never have to work another day in his life, but Arthur did not feel much like a success that day.

The day before, Arthur had buried his wife. With no children and no real friends, Arthur felt alone. But Arthur made a decision that day, a decision that would change his life. Arthur went for a drive.

God truly accompanied Arthur that day. As Arthur parked his Rolls Royce and got out to take a stroll in the park, he was oblivious to all those people who seemed to be having a good time. That is until a little boy walked by with his mother and changed Arthur's life forever.

The little boy was singing, but it was what he was singing that changed Arthur. As the little boy sang "Jesus loves me this I know," tears began to flow down Arthur's cheeks. Arthur was so moved that he returned to his car and began to sing the song that his mother sang to him when he was a little boy.

Arthur knew that Jesus loved him, but as other things took over his time and his mind, he forgot about Jesus. Arthur decided that he would never forget that Jesus loved him, and he would do his best to make sure that no one else forgot either.

A short time later Arthur opened an ice cream store, but this was no ordinary ice cream store. Above the awning were the words Jesus' Ice Cream Store, and the sign on the window read: "Free Ice Cream: You Must Be Under Age 21 Or Feel Like You

Haven't A Friend In The World In Order To Receive Free Ice Cream."

Only God knows how many people Arthur has led to accept Jesus Christ as their Savior. Arthur shared his story with anyone who was willing to listen as they licked their cone. As each customer stared through the case and decided what flavor they wanted that day, they could not help but hear the song playing in the background, "Jesus Loves Me This I Know." Arthur knows because a little boy told him so.

No Room

It was the Saturday after Thanksgiving. Everyone in the Abbott family was excited. That was the day they always put up their Christmas decorations. Each family member knew his or her specific job. Mr. Abbott and Tommy put up the outdoor decorations. Mrs. Abbott put up the tree and wrapped all of the presents, and Heather did the rest of the indoor decorating. The Abbotts started early because it was so time consuming.

"Lunch is ready. Everybody come and get it," Mrs. Abbott hollered after everyone had put in a few hours doing their jobs.

"How's it going, guys?" she asked when Tommy and his dad came to the table.

"Pretty good, hon. We have the lights strung most of the way around the house. We still have to put the blinking lights on the bushes and put up the yard displays," her husband answered.

"Yeah, Dad, and don't forget we need to put Santa and the reindeer up on the roof," Tommy added.

"I'm not forgetting, Son. Remember, I was doing this before you were born."

"Yeah, I know," Tommy replied, "only back then the roof was steeper and there was always a blinding snowstorm."

"How did you know?" his dad responded.

"Okay, guys. Enough about your stuff. Does anyone want to know what I've accomplished?" Mrs. Abbott asked.

"Only if it involved wrapping a lot of presents for me," Tommy replied.

"You? What about me?" Heather asked.

"Okay! Okay! Wait a minute. My turn again. I've almost finished putting all the ornaments on the tree. After I finish that, all I have to do is put the icicles on it and spray it with snow."

"Is that all you've done, Mom?" Tommy asked.

"Is that all? It's a big tree. And I don't have a helper like you do. And when I finish this I have to wrap all the presents."

"Like I said, be sure and wrap a lot for me," Tommy replied. Mrs. Abbott thought about all the presents she had to wrap.

"I sure hope the kids like all of the video games, computer software, and designer clothes I got them, and I hope Roger likes all of his new tools and hunting and fishing gear. After all, these things were not cheap. It is a good thing I had all of those credit cards," Mrs. Abbott thought to herself.

"And when I finish wrapping all our stuff, I have to wrap everything I bought everyone else. Everyone had better spend as much on us as I spent on them."

"Earth to Mom!" Heather called out.

"Did you say something, Heather?"

"Yes, Mom. While you were daydreaming."

"Sorry, dear. What was it you wanted?"

"Don't I get a chance to brag about what all I've done, too?" Heather asked.

"Of course, dear," her mother replied.

"Well, I've been putting out all the Santas, elves, reindeer, candy canes, stockings and other Christmas items," Heather replied triumphantly.

"Yeah, but look at how much you have left to do," Tommy added.

"But I'm almost out of space, little boy," his sister replied.

"Don't *little boy*, me. I'm doing a man's work," Tommy shot back.

"Whatever!" Heather replied.

By late afternoon, everything appeared to be done. The guys had all of the decorations up and all of the lights working. Mrs. Abbott had wrapped everything and put it under the tree. There was hardly anywhere to walk. All that remained was putting the empty boxes that stored the decorations back in the attic until it was time to put everything away for another year.

"Hey, what's this? It still has stuff in it," Mr. Abbott said.

"Look! It's Jesus, Mary, Joseph, shepherds, wise men, and animals," said Tommy. "We have to put them out!"

"Yeah, but there's no place to put them," Heather replied.

"She's right about that," Mrs. Abbott said.

Everyone felt bad because there was no room for the nativity scene, but no one had a suggestion. Finally, someone came up with the idea to make sure they included the Jesus decorations the next year. Everyone was afraid they would forget, so they taped a big note on the top of the box: JESUS, NEXT YEAR. Then, they all felt better.

Only One

Mary sat in a chair. She was exhausted. It had been a long couple of days, or had it been longer? Mary looked at her son, Tommy, who was across the room. Mary felt the effects of her medication and the rigors of her plight. Tommy seemed a blur to her.

Mary's pastor had just left. Had he really spent two hours with her after preaching Mrs. Haley's funeral earlier that day?

Mary appreciated her pastor. He did his best to reassure her than nothing that happened was her fault, but she would always wonder. What could she have done differently? What could she have done so that none of this would have happened? She had tried to raise Tommy the best she could. Would things have been different if her husband had not died when Tommy was a small boy?

Mary's thoughts returned to her pastor. He was the only one who came. The only one! None of her friends came. None of Tommy's friends came. Mary wanted to think it was because none of them had any answers to give her, rather than think they had abandoned her. Maybe Mary's friends felt it would have been hard on her to face them. It would have. It was hard for Mary to face herself.

The next day would be even harder on Mary. Would anyone come? Would anyone be there when she needed them? Her pastor would be there, but would anyone else? And would he still preach Tommy's funeral if no one came?

It had to be tough on Mary's pastor. Pastors always say nice things about the deceased, but what could he say good about Tommy? After all, Tommy had murdered Mrs. Haley, lovable old Mrs. Haley.

Was it better this way? Was it better that Tommy fired at the policemen who caught him coming out of Mrs. Haley's house?

Maybe in time Mary would have some answers, but she was too exhausted to think of answers that night. All that she could remember was that only one person had come for her that day. Only one. Only her pastor. But then she remembered that only one had been there for her before. Only one had died for her that day on Calvary, and in that case only one was enough.

Easter Morning

Five-year-old Johnny remembered nothing good about Good Friday. Johnny went to the store with his father. A car's brakes screeched as Johnny's father headed across the parking lot, but the driver could not stop soon enough.

"Get up, Daddy! Get up!" Johnny cried as he bent over his father, who lay motionless in the parking lot.

Neither Johnny nor his mother Karen felt like taking part in the church's Easter egg hunt the next day, but on Sunday morning Karen knew where she and Johnny needed to be.

"Come on, Johnny! Time to get up! We have to go to church for the Easter sunrise service."

Karen knew church was where they would receive the most comfort, and comfort was what both of them needed at that time. Some people from their church would be at the funeral home that evening, but Karen needed someone that morning, and so did Johnny.

Karen and Johnny struggled to get ready and arrived at the outdoor service just as it began.

As the pastor finished his message, the sun peeped over the horizon. Almost immediately, people started coming up to Karen and Johnny offering their condolences.

As Karen looked at Johnny, she noticed a change in him.

"I guess these hugs must have had an effect on Johnny. He almost looks like he's smiling," Karen thought to herself.

Karen took Johnny home for some much needed rest between the sunrise service and the regular service, only to return for the pastor's second message of the day.

"Let's hurry to that place where daddy was last night," Johnny told his mother.

"We'll leave in a few minutes," Karen replied, puzzled by his request.

When they arrived at the funeral home, Johnny bounded out of the car and headed inside. His mother strained in order to keep up with him.

Johnny hurried into the room where his father lay, looked up, and came to an abrupt halt. Johnny froze and his tears began to flow. After a few moments, Johnny inched toward the casket, and stretched up to whisper in his father's ear.

"Daddy, if Jesus could come back, why can't you?"

Johnny felt an arm on his shoulder. His mother tried her best to console him, and he turned to face her.

After they embraced for a few minutes, Johnny broke the silence. "Well, if I can't have my Daddy, I'm glad Jesus got him."

Dear Linda

Linda felt as if life had thrown her into the pits. A short time later, it seemed like someone yanked her out of the pits and tossed her in quicksand.

Linda's automobile accident left her paralyzed from the waist down. Since her mother quit speaking to her years before when she married David, David seemed to be all Linda had, and "had" seemed to be the appropriate word.

A hospital employee handed Linda an envelope. She recognized the handwriting. She could not figure out why David had not come to the hospital that day, nor why he sent her a note. Linda opened the envelope and began reading.

Dear Linda,

I hate to tell you this way, but I don't see any other way. You know it devastated me when you told me the doctor said you couldn't have children. You know how much I want children.

I almost left you then, and I should have, but I decided to hang in there and give it a try. You can't blame me for wanting out. You know how much I love sports and how I want a son so I can teach him how to play baseball.

Well, last month I met Debonee. Debonee's divorced and has a son who would love for me to teach him how to play baseball. As a matter of fact, I've already been teaching him.

Oh, Debonee and I haven't done anything wrong. That is unless you can call a little kiss every now and then wrong.

I wish I'd left you before your accident. Now, you'll blame all of this on the accident, and I guess the accident does have something to do with it, but the accident happened after I met Debonee and Jason.

Jason needs me. His father died a couple of years ago. Oh, I know you think you need me, too, but you're really better off without me. You'll be all right. The doctor will help you with a rehabilitation program, and I know you'll make some new friends there. You need friends who are like you are. Those are the best kind of friends for you right now.

I'll send you some money until you get on your feet, and....

Linda heard a knock at the door. She looked up from the note and did her best to wipe the tears from her eyes before anyone could see her.

"Yes," Linda called out.

The door opened and in walked a gray-haired woman.

"Mom! Is that you?"

Alive Again

Albee loved it when John pushed her wheelchair down the hill near their home. They did this a lot. Albee could talk her big brother into just about anything.

Albee loved it when John would let go, let her ride on her own, and catch the chair just before they got to the bottom of the hill.

It was okay. There was no traffic on the street and John always managed to catch her in time. At least, all except that one last time.

A stranger had turned onto their street by mistake. He never saw the wheelchair until after he heard it and heard Albee's screams. Not only did Albee's life end that day, John's did, too. At least it did for a while.

John was lost without Albee and began to withdraw. He blamed himself for Albee's death. The boy who was once the life of the party became the sullen recluse who could care less about anything or anyone.

John quit going to church, forgot about any dreams he had for college or a career, and finished high school doing just enough to get by and get out.

He took a small apartment, where he spent all of his days. He found a job as a night watchman. The job enabled him to pay the bills and avoid people.

Few people planned a career as a night watchman, but to John it was the perfect career. He could be miserable. He had plenty of time to beat himself up and knock himself down.

No one interfered. His father left home after he found out Albee would never walk and his mother died of a broken heart after Albee died and John withdrew.

Eric, John's best friend from childhood, managed to track him down. John was not pleased to see Eric, because Eric represented the fun times, and John did not allow himself any pleasant memories. Eric was determined to get back into John's life.

It took many months before John began to open up a little. After a while John agreed to go to church with Eric. He did not know why he agreed to go, but he did.

Little by little, God used Eric to work in John's life. Finally Eric was able to convince John into going on a Christian men's weekend. A previous weekend changed Eric's life.

John had a wonderful weekend. When John left that weekend, he left something behind. He left behind his guilt. John offered his guilt to Jesus and Jesus took it. Jesus forgave John and convinced John to forgive himself. Once again, John was alive!

Used Reference

"Don't open them until I'm gone." The stranger spoke those words as he handed a Bible to everyone in the church.

Angie looked down at the Bible the stranger had given her. Some of the Bibles looked almost new. Not hers. Angie held a Bible worn at the corners and cracked from many years of use.

"Why didn't I get an almost new one like everyone else? Look at the one Phyllis got. Why Phyllis's Bible looks like it hasn't even been opened. How come I didn't get one like that?"

Angie looked at Willie. As the stranger looked over the congregation, he noticed Willie had no Bible. He reached in his box and handed Willie a brand new one.

"Hmmm! Why can't I have a new one like Willie?" Angie wondered.

Then Angie noticed the Bible the stranger gave the pastor. It looked like it had been taped and glued together more than once.

"Well, at least my Bible looks better than one person's Bible," Angie thought to herself.

"Please bow your heads with me," the stranger instructed everyone.

Angie bowed briefly, then opened her eyes to look at the stranger.

"Where is he? He's gone. But he couldn't have left. He didn't have time to get out the door," Angie thought to herself.

"Where did he go?" Angie asked out loud, forgetting for a moment that she was in church.

Everyone opened his or her eyes when they heard Angie exclaim. They began to look for the stranger, but he could not be found.

"Where did he go?" someone else repeated.

After a search proved futile, someone gasped, and then another person gasped.

Angie looked and saw that both of them had opened their Bibles. Others opened their Bibles and gasped as well.

Angie opened her Bible and she gasped, too. The Bible contained her grandmother's name and a date a long time ago. As Angie leafed through the Bible she noticed a lot of writing, all of it in her grandmother's handwriting.

"But how did the stranger get hold of my grandmother's Bible?"

Tears streamed down Angie's face. No longer did she want to trade her Bible for another one. By the look on the faces of the others in her church, Angie assumed that they, too, had Bibles of loved ones, and none of them wanted to exchange their Bible for a new one, either.

Everyone held a Bible belonging to a loved one except Willie. Willie had a new Bible. Willie was an eight-year-old orphan whose parents died the week he was born.

After everyone took a few moments to look through the Bibles the stranger had given them, they began to gather and talk.

"Who was this stranger?" they asked.

No one could agree what the stranger looked like.

"I think he's a construction worker," Willie said.

"Why would you say that, Willie?" Angie asked.

"Because his hands were all scarred."

Going Home

Martha sat in her chair and stared straight ahead. She rose before the sun, or at least before the sun usually rose. The darkness outside symbolized Martha's day, because the clouds of the previous day engulfed her life and swallowed every ray of sunshine.

The day before Martha awoke full of sunshine and joy, because her son, his wife, and their children were coming home after six long years out west. Home to stay, but not in the way Martha wanted.

It seemed so long ago that Martha excitedly hollered out, "Just a minute!" when she heard a knock at the door.

She expected a hoard of embraces. Martha's demeanor changed quickly when she noticed the policeman.

"Yes?" Martha whispered, already afraid.

The policeman spoke the words that Martha would remember forever.

"Are you Mrs. Sullivan? Mrs. Martha Sullivan?"

Martha nodded and the policeman continued.

"I'm sorry to have to tell you this, but there's been an accident. I'm sorry, but there were no survivors."

"My...my son?" Martha asked.

"I'm afraid so. A man had a heart attack, which caused a tractor trailer to plow into his car and lose its load. This caused your son's car to slide over the spillage and down a steep embankment. I'm sorry I had to bring you this kind of news. Is there anything I can do for you before I leave?"

Martha shook her head, and the policeman turned to leave.

Gone was Martha's opportunity to get to know her grandchildren. No more visits, no more pictures, no more e-mail messages, and no phone calls. Martha would not be able to make up for lost time with her son. She would not have a chance to be a mother to her daughter-in-law, whose own mother had died.

Martha began making phone calls. Friends from church came over when they heard the news. While her friends comforted her, they could never make up for the family Martha would no longer have.

Almost everyone said, "I'll pray for you," and some even prayed with Martha before they left. Prayer had helped Martha get on with her life after her husband died, but this time it was different. Martha expected her son, daughter-in-law, and grandchildren to stand over her casket some day, not the other way around.

"Caskets!" Even the thought of it made Martha shudder, but she had to make funeral arrangements.

"We'll go with you," her friends Ruth and Laura said.

"It's good to have friends at a time like this. Thanks."

Martha knew countless others would be at the funeral. But what about after the funeral? People usually forget in a few days, or at least a few weeks. Friends have to get back to their lives. Eventually, they leave and loneliness moves in to stay.

But all of this happened the day before. Martha sat and stared, oblivious to the fact that most of the world was going on in a normal fashion.

In the midst of her long morning of mourning, the sound of the doorbell brought Martha back to the world around her.

"Who could that be? Ruth and Laura are not due for another forty-five minutes."

Martha stood up and headed to the front door. She opened it and stared at the stranger facing her.

"Are you Martha Sullivan?" the stranger asked, reminding Martha of the words that led to the terrible news of the day before.

"Y-yes," Martha stuttered.

"I'm Bob Mitchell. You don't know me, but it was my dad who had the heart attack yesterday that caused your family's deaths. I know 'I'm sorry' isn't enough, but I don't know what else to say. I lost my mom and dad yesterday, just like you lost your family."

As Martha watched the tears stream down this young man's face, she forgot about herself. She thought of Jesus and invited the young man inside.

The Least Of These

The shopkeeper looked up, startled by the ringing of the bell as someone entered his store. He did not expect anyone to venture out on this snowy day. His surprised look soon turned to a frown as his eyes landed on the unkempt man standing in front of him.

"M..m..may I help you with something?" the shopkeeper asked.

"Uh, I was wondering if you could spare a quarter for a cup of coffee," the man replied.

"I'm sorry, but I make it a point never to give money to beggars. You might try the church. That's where I give my money."

"Well, thank you anyway," the stranger replied as he turned to exit.

As the stranger left, the shopkeeper thought some more.

"Maybe this guy was on the up and up, and he only wanted a quarter. Still, if I gave him a quarter this time he'd just come back again and want more next time. However, a quarter won't hurt."

The shopkeeper continued wrestling with his conscience until he convinced himself to give the beggar a quarter. Having done so, he walked to the door, opened it, and was hit by a gust of wind.

The shopkeeper looked up and down the street, but saw no trace of the man who had only moments before left his store. Not only that, but he spotted no tracks heading toward or away from his establishment. Puzzled, he closed the door and once again stepped behind the counter.

"Maybe he tried the store next door. I'll call Josh and see."

"Cravett's," a voice answered.

"Hi, Josh. This is Levi next door."

"Oh, hi Levi. What do you think about this weather?"

"A little rough for me. I'm counting the days until spring, but I don't want to talk about the weather right now, Josh. I have a question. Do you have anyone in the store at the moment?"

"Actually, Levi, this is the first time today I haven't had anyone in the store. Why do you ask?"

"Well, I just had some homeless guy in here asking for a quarter. He didn't happen to stop by your place, too, did he?"

"No, but I did have one yesterday, Levi."

"Did he happen to have a burgundy stocking cap pulled way down and have a scraggly beard?"

"Sounds just like my guy. You say he stopped by your place today?"

"Yeah! Sounds like he's making his rounds. Josh, did you give him any money when he stopped in yesterday?"

"Yeah, I felt so sorry for him that I gave him two quarters, and not only that, but I gave him a piece of cake and some hot chocolate. You'll never believe what happened after that."

"He didn't try to rob you, did he, Josh?"

"No, nothing like that, Levi. Remember how hard it snowed yesterday? Well, it was a little after noon when he came in and he was the first person to open my door all day."

"Yeah, same for me today, Josh."

"Yeah, but after he left, I had all kinds of business, and several of them said they had never heard of my business until this homeless guy told them about me. Funny thing is that most of my customers were well dressed. They didn't even look like someone who would give a homeless man the time of day. And today's been more of the same."

"You mean you've had lots of customers, or that the customers you've had told you a homeless guy sent them?"

"Both."

"If he happens to come back, Josh, could you send him back over here?"

"In others words, you didn't give him any money."

Separable Twins

Twins Ron and Don were alike. Both were always involved in everything in school. Both became successful in business. Each was blessed with a miserable wife who raised their children. Ron and Don seldom spent time with their families, because they were too busy taking care of their clients. Ron and Don spoke to civic groups and attended their clients' parties.

Occasionally, Ron and Don attended church. If something happened which prevented them from making it to their children's birthday parties, they stopped and got a nice gift to make everything right. The same was true for missed ball games and dance recitals. They were proud of their children.

When Ron and Don celebrated their thirty-seventh birthday, they took time to talk on the phone and wish each other a blessed event. They claimed it would be different when they celebrated their fortieth birthdays. They would allow their wives to throw them a surprise birthday party, and they would take the time to attend.

But for one of them, that fortieth birthday never came. One night, Don sat quietly in a well upholstered chair with his head bowed while Ron lay in a casket not too far away.

As Don sat with his head bowed and his hands folded together, he began to think of all that he had missed in his thirty-seven years. He vowed that the next day he would begin a life anew.

Six months later, would he still take time for God and family or would the memories of his brother have faded? Would he resume his busy lifestyle? And if he did, would he get back on track by his next birthday when no one called to wish him a happy birthday?

Dan's Anniversary Present

Dan awakened early one Saturday morning, realized it was his anniversary and pulled the pillow over his face.

"Some anniversary," he thought. "Just like last year."

Just as he had every morning for the past year and a half, Dan looked over at the empty space in the bed next to him. The last eighteen months had been tough on Dan. He only felt numbness and pain.

"Oh to hear Molly's voice again," he had thought oh so many times.

Many times he had replayed that night in his mind. Dan had worked late that night. He had called Molly to tell her he had to finish a project before he came home. Dan was always thoughtful enough to let Molly know if he would be late.

Dan had been working hard for several weeks. Molly decided to fix him his favorite dish, lasagna, for dinner. She realized that she was out of something she needed for it and headed off to the store to buy it. She never returned.

Soon after Dan got home, a policeman pulled up in front of Dan's house. Dan knew something had to be wrong.

"Are you Dan Larkins?" the policeman asked.

"Yes, is something wrong?"

"I'm afraid there is. There's been an accident. The rain-soaked streets caused your wife to slide into a semi."

"Is...is she...."

"No, she isn't dead. But she's at Randolph Memorial in pretty bad shape. Shall I give you an escort?"

"That would be great."

Shortly after Dan arrived at the hospital Dr. Reyes came out to talk to him.

"How's my wife? Can I see her?"

"In a minute Mr. Larkins. Your wife has some bruises and a few broken bones, but as far as we can tell she does not have

170

any internal injuries. However, she's in a coma and there's no telling if or when she'll come out of it."

A year and a half later Molly still had not come out of the coma. At first, people tried to comfort Dan by telling him how lucky Molly was to be alive, but after a few weeks nobody bothered to say that.

Every day after work Dan headed to convalescent hospital to spend a few minutes with Molly and talk to her. It was hard on Dan to talk to Molly when she could not answer him. Dr. Reyes had told Dan that people in comas can sometimes hear what you tell them. Dan hoped that his daily visit would help Molly come out of the coma.

At least Dan used to hope. In recent months, it had taken all the strength Dan could muster just to get him to the hospital each day. It helped Dan that Dr. Reyes had not given up hope and continued to see Molly.

As Dan lay on the bed trying to decide whether to get up and shower, the phone rang.

"Dan."

"Yes, this is Dan. Who's this?"

"Dan, this is Dr. Reyes."

"It's about Molly, isn't it, doctor? She's gone, isn't she?"

"No, Dan! Quite the opposite! Are you sitting down? Someone wants to talk to you."

"Dan, it's me, Molly. Dr. Reyes said today's our anniversary. Happy Anniversary, Dan."

As Dan listened, tears streamed down his cheeks. "Happy anniversary, indeed. God has given me the most wonderful anniversary present anyone could give. A present only He could give."

Just The Four Of Us

Five-year-old Todd watched his mother Debbie walk down the aisle toward him. She looked pretty in her new dress. As she got closer Todd could see that she was smiling and crying at the same time. "Was she happy or sad?" he wondered.

Debbie used to cry all the time back when she lived with Todd's father. Todd's father was abusive.

Todd clutched the ring bearer pillow with both hands. He thought he was too big to be a ring bearer, but his mother insisted that he do it. Todd wanted to please his mother because he loved her very much.

Todd worried about losing his mother. She was all he had. He did not have any friends and his grandparents lived so far away.

Todd used to be with his mother all the time but that was before she met Mark. Lately Debbie and Mark had been going out by themselves a lot or too busy planning the wedding to spend time with Todd.

Debbie said it would be different after she and Mark married, but Todd was not sure. Every time Debbie and Mark went out, Todd had to stay with Mrs. Lefferts. Todd liked Mrs. Lefferts, but she was not his mother.

Todd watched as his mother drew closer, but she did not look at him. Debbie looked at Mark. Todd was glad that his mother seemed to be happy, but he felt left out.

When Debbie stopped walking, the preacher started talking. Todd moved back-and-forth from one foot to the other. On the one hand, he felt like everyone was looking at him. On the other hand, he was afraid they were not looking at him. He wanted to get this over with before he dropped the ring.

As Debbie and Mark went from standing to kneeling, Todd could not help but wonder if things would be different.

Todd hoped Mark would not make his mother cry the way his dad did and he hoped his mother would still take time to hold him the way she used to.

Todd became so engrossed in contemplating his future that he almost did not hear his cue. They practiced so much the night before. He did not want to mess up in front of everyone. The church was full this time. Many of those in attendance were people from the church, while others were friends and relatives of Mark's, most of whom came from out of town.

Todd was not sure how much he was going to like church. He had not been used to going to church. They never went when he and his mother lived with his dad.

Todd decided to wait and see what he thought of church after he lived with Mark a while, because it was at this church that his mother met Mark.

Todd remembered they met in something called a "singles class." Todd was not sure what that was. He just knew that Mark had never been married.

Todd looked up just in time to see his mother kiss Mark. Todd remembered how his mother would always hold him and kiss him, particularly after they left his dad. Todd hoped she would still take time to hold him and kiss him.

Todd stood there as someone started to play music again. Debbie and Mark turned and started to walk down the aisle. They had gone only a couple of steps when Mark said something to Debbie and the two of them stopped. Mark let go of new bride's hand and turned around and looked at Todd.

"Come on, Tiger," Mark called out to him, as he held out his hand.

Todd needed no more urging and ran up to them. Then, the three of them walked down the aisle with Todd in the middle.

"Maybe, things will be different this time," he thought.

When they got to the end of the aisle, Mark lifted Todd.

"From now on, Tiger, it's just the four of us -- you, me, your mother, and Jesus." Mark said.

Grandma's Quilts

Eight-year old Sarah climbed the steps to her grandparents' attic. Her gait was much slower than when she descended those same steps that morning as her flaxen-colored hair bounced with each step.

Halfway up the stairs Sarah turned and looked at her grandmother moving slowly up the stairs behind her.

"Do you want me to help you, grandma?" Sarah asked, concerned about her grandmother.

"No, I'm fine, Sarah. I'm just a little slow this time of day."

While the time of day was not late for the city people in Sarah's neighborhood, most of Sarah's neighbors did not rise at 4:30 a.m. the way her grandparents did.

When Sarah and her grandmother had successfully navigated all the steps, Sarah waited for her grandmother to rest a moment and then headed to her bed away from home, where she looked forward to sleeping under her grandmother's quilts.

Since the attic had no source of heat, Sarah needed many quilts to keep warm each time she made her winter visit. Sarah and her brothers visited their grandparents one at a time. Each of them visited for a week in the summer and a few days during the winter, as well as those times when the entire family visited.

"Grandma, I like it when I can come and spend some time with you and grandpa. I'm so glad you live close enough that I can come often."

"I'm glad we do, too, Sarah, and I'm glad we can have you, Tommy, and Billy, come and see us one at a time, so we can give each of you some of our time."

"Time enough to spoil us, huh, grandma?"

"Probably so, but not rotten."

"I like coming here, even if you do put me to work."

"A little hard work never hurt anyone, Sarah. Always remember that."

"Oh, I will. Besides, my friends think it's cool that I get to help you and grandpa feed the pigs, milk the cows, collect the eggs from the chickens, and pick food from the garden in the summer, but none of that is my favorite reason for coming."

"And what is, Sarah?"

"Well, actually spending time with you and grandpa, but next to that, getting to come up here and sleep under all these quilts. I feel like this is my special place, and while the room is chilly, I stay nice and warm under all these quilts. Oh, I know I have the quilt at home that you made for me, and I love it, but there's something special about sleeping under the quilts at your house. Did you make all these quilts, grandma?"

"Some of them, but some of them were made by my mama, and grandma."

"They must be really old!"

"They are, Sarah. I remember when I was your age I watched mama and grandma making quilts. They made quilts for everyone. They even let me help a little, and of course, I helped more when I got older."

"Wow, can I help you make a quilt sometime?"

"Maybe, sometime, but my hands won't let me make as many quilts as I used to."

"Well, I'm really glad God let you make one for me."

"Me, too, Sarah. See this quilt?"

"Of course, grandma."

"I can still remember what my mama said to me the day she finished it."

"What's that, grandma?"

"She said 'Ethel, see this here quilt?' Mama never had much education, so she talked a little different. Anyway, I said, 'Yes, mama.'

"Mama said, 'Do you think it's pretty?'

"I said, 'It's beautiful, mama,' and mama said, 'Do you know why it's beautiful, Ethel?'

"And I said, 'Because you made it, mama.'

175

"And she said, 'No, Ethel. It's 'cause of all these different kinds of material and colors.' 'Ethel,' she said. 'It's just like people. The more kinds of people and the more different colors of people you have in your life, the better your life will be.

"'Ethel', she said. 'Always remember this. Ain't no person no better than no other person. It don't matter what color skin they have, how pretty they are, or how much money they have, 'cause God made all of them, just like I made all of this quilt, and God made all of them special.'

"Sarah, mama was right. The more different people you meet and make friends with in life, the better your life, because God made everyone, and God made everyone special. Always remember that, Sarah."

"I'll try, grandma, but it's still hard for me to believe."

"What's hard for you to believe, Sarah?"

"That everyone's as special as you are."

The Not-So-Odd Couple

Many said the term "odd couple" must have been coined for Henry and Martha. Some people said they could not imagine how Henry and Martha had gotten together. Others said that God was responsible, and He had kept them together for forty-seven years.

Henry and Martha were always together. Each Sunday morning they sat in one of the front pews of the church. Henry always complimented the pastor on his sermon.

Each night, when the weather was good, Henry latched onto Martha's arm and they strolled through the neighborhood. Theirs was an older neighborhood. Each house had a big porch. Many neighbors sat on their porch swings and called out to Henry and Martha. Martha always waved to them. Each time someone greeted them, Henry's face broke out into a big smile, and he lifted his head and returned a cheerful "hello."

When they returned home, Henry and Martha turned on their TV. Martha loved the silent comedies of Buster Keaton, Harold Lloyd, and Charlie Chaplin. Henry liked serious drama. One night Martha chose the movie. The next night Henry selected it. They never argued over whose turn it was. No one had heard Henry and Martha argue, not even their children.

While Martha did not need the closed captioning on her silent movies, she did when watching Henry's dramas. Martha was never blessed with the ability to hear.

Henry was thankful for the SAP button which gave him a thorough description of what was happening. He never received the gift of sight.

Henry and Martha always chuckled when they told others about their nightly dates. Those people could never understand how Henry and Martha could enjoy movies.

Each night they took in a movie before they headed to bed. Before turning in, Henry and Martha knelt together and said their prayers. They were so thankful for all God had given them. They thought God had given them much more than He had given most people.

Stan's Puzzle Lesson

"Okay, everybody! Listen up! We have a project that we'll be working on together for the next several weeks. That means all of us all have to work together. I need to go over a few things with you before we start."

"Lesson number one. How many people does it take to make a marriage?" Stan asked.

"I'm not going to have to marry you, am I, Stan?" Ed asked, as everyone else in the room laughed.

"Ed, I know your wife. She's excited that I'll have you many nights over the next few weeks so she can have some peace and quiet. She knows it takes two to make a good marriage. A wife and her mother."

Everyone laughed as Stan continued.

"Okay, everyone, how many of you think Ed's wife has it easy, raise your hand? Notice the absence of hands, everyone.

"You only have to please one other person to make a marriage work. Here, you'll have to please a lot more, so let me educate you a little."

"This is a piece of a jigsaw puzzle," Stan continued.

"Could you go a little slower, Stan?" Mary chimed in.

"Well, look at the group I have," Stan replied. "Now, I'm sure that all of you have worked a jigsaw puzzle at one time or another, so all of you know that it takes many pieces to make up a puzzle. Now try to think of all of us as the pieces of the puzzle. Just as each puzzle piece is different, so are all of us different from each other."

"Viva la difference," Norman shouted.

"Hear, hear," Lois agreed.

"May you still be praising the difference a couple of weeks from now. Now, if I can have your attention, I'll get back to educating you about your similarity to a puzzle piece," Stan said, getting the group back to his lesson. "Some of you are like the edge pieces of a puzzle. You give structure to the project. We need structure so that our project will be completed. We can't have things going all over the place.

"Others of you are like the colorful pieces that make up the central part of the puzzle. You like to have fun and call attention to yourself. The world would be a mighty boring place without you.

"Still others of you are like the pieces that make up the sky and grass in the puzzle. You don't give them a lot of thought, but they are instrumental in seeing that the project is completed.

"Then there are those dark pieces. People who represent the dark pieces of a puzzle are those who question everything. While we don't need a lot of them, we do need some people like that in order to make sure we are on the right track.

"As you can see, just as a puzzle needs all those different puzzle pieces so that the puzzle can come together, we need all of you different types of people to see that this project will be completed. To put this in a Christian perspective, we each have different gifts and talents and all of them are needed.

"Yes, each of you are needed. It's possible before our work is done, someone will drive you nuts, but just stay calm. Chances are you're driving him or her just as nuts. Imagine how God must feel each time we do something that's not what He wants us to do.

"Now, so that none of us forget, I'm going to give each of you four puzzle pieces, plus I'm going to leave one of each piece up front on the table. Anytime someone is about to drive you nuts, reach in your pocket or purse and pull out the puzzle piece that best describes him or her. Just pull it out, look at it, and shake your head. By the way, you don't need to open your mouth to shake your head. If all of us keep a positive focus, we'll accomplish our goal and remain friends. Now, any questions?

"Yes, Linda."

"Do you have enough puzzle pieces that I give Ed's wife one of each and explain to her what they mean?"

"Good idea, Linda, but I think someone has already given her a set. I saw her looking at Ed the other day and she just shook her head."

The Twelfth Day

Monica tossed and turned. It was that way every year. Monica had trouble sleeping on the night before the "twelfth day." She looked over at Brad, who was sleeping like a baby just like he always had been able to do.

Monica turned and looked at the clock. It read 2:37.

"Is that all?" Monica thought. "It should be later than that."

Monica tried to get to sleep, but to no avail. Her mind raced as she wondered what was in store for her the next day.

Ever since she and Brad had gotten serious, he used his love for Monica and his love for Christmas and giving to institute the Brad Conwell Twelve Days Of Christmas Giving. There were no Scrooges in his family. It was a good thing Brad could afford to spoil Monica.

After they married, he spoiled her even more. Brad always started small. Well, small as far as Brad was concerned. Brad always gave Monica something inexpensive for the house on the first day, and the last day was always something unpredictable, but wonderful.

"Wonder what it could be?" Monica thought, knowing sleep would be out of the question again this year.

Monica thought back to all the presents Brad had gotten her. Her favorite was the time he sent Monica and her best friend from childhood on a shopping spree to New York City. Monica enjoyed the shopping spree, but she loved her time with her best friend even more.

Monica's mind raced more quickly than the clock, but eventually the numbers on the clock reached 6:00, and the alarm began to sound.

"Time to get up, Brad! Come on, Brad! Rise and shine!"

"Just give me another couple of hours sleep," Brad replied, wanting to have fun at his wife's expense. Brad never woke up tired, a trait his wife wished she had.

"Oh, no you don't! Where's my present?" Monica asked.

"Present? Oh, yeah. Don't you remember? I gave it to you yesterday."

"That was present number eleven and you know it."

"Eleven? Are you sure?" Brad asked.

"Yes, and you know it, too! Now where's my present?"

"Oh, now I remember. I decided that due to the financial crisis I would only give you eleven presents this year. You'd better watch yourself. I may cut back to ten next year."

"And I may hide your golf clubs this spring. Now, where is it?"

"Okay, let's get dressed and go downstairs."

"And why do we have to get dressed, Brad? Is it in the driveway this time?"

"That's for me to know and you to find out. Now if you want your last present, you need to play by my rules."

"Okay, you've got the upper hand. Now out of bed and get dressed."

Monica dressed quickly and waited for Brad who seemed to be prolonging her agony.

"Hurry up, slow poke."

"Okay, let's go. I'm ready," Brad said. "Now, down to the living room."

Monica raced down the stairs and turned to face her husband who seemed to be taking his one step at a time a little slower than normal.

"Is this it?" Monica asked, as she spotted a white box with red ribbon.

"Yes, but sit down first, and you have to sit on the sofa."

"It matters where I sit?" Monica asked.

"It sure does, so take a seat little lady."

"Aye, aye, sir," Monica said as she saluted her husband.

Possessing no lady-like skills at that moment, Monica tore through the paper, ripped open the box, and looked at what looked like a photograph album.

Puzzled, she took it out of the box and opened it to the first page, surprised that she found nothing. Since she knew her husband's clever nature she turned to the next page, and then the next. Still, she found nothing other than plastic sheets where she could display photographs.

"Okay, Smarty Pants. Where's the rest of it?" Monica asked.

"If I were you I'd keep turning," Brad replied.

Monica turned another page and then another. Near the back Monica finally found a brochure advertising a cabin in the mountains.

"When are we going?" Monica asked. "And how long will we be gone?"

"You will be gone for two weeks. I will not be going at all," Brad replied.

Monica had lived with Brad long enough that she knew the next page might produce another clue, but she was not prepared for what she would find.

"Where did you get this, Brad?" This is a picture of my sister Melanie whom I haven't seen since we left the orphanage. Who is this woman in the other picture? Oh my gosh...Oh my gosh...It's... It's....

"It's me," whispered a voice behind her. Monica wheeled around and began to weep uncontrollably as her sister rushed around the sofa and embraced her.

It Was A Good Sunday

It was a good Sunday. Pastor Prime looked out at the congregation. He did not like Sundays when the congregation came disguised as empty seats. He wanted them elbow-to-elbow. It was an elbow-to-elbow Sunday. It was a Sunday to make them squirm in their seats. That made it a good Sunday. Although it was not Easter, Pastor Prime chose to preach on the resurrection, the resurrection most people lived.

"And they took Jesus' body and laid it in the tomb and sealed it. The End," Pastor Prime said as he planted the hook.

He paused and looked up at the congregation. They knew it was coming. It was always coming. Maybe that was the reason they kept coming.

"You mean it wasn't the end? You look like it was. You came in today just as if you arrived at the funeral home to see Jesus. I already called. Jesus isn't at the funeral home. Jesus was never at the funeral home. Jesus is alive! How is it the song goes? 'He's alive! He's alive! He's alive and I'm forgiven! Heaven's gates are open wide!' It's almost enough to make you want to tell someone, isn't it? Yeah, I know. Almost, but not quite," Pastor Prime went on.

Pastor Prime paused hoping for an amen, but all he got was a small cough by one nervous parishioner.

"People, nowhere in the Bible does it say 'Thou shalt not take God with you when you leave the church.' You don't have to leave Jesus at the church when you leave each week. You can take him with you. You can share him with those you see each day.

"You think it's okay to mention Jesus here after you see what everyone is wearing and talk about the ballgame. Why don't you mention him to those you know who don't come here to church? Are you afraid they don't believe in God?

"Mr. Potter, do you know your boss believes in God? He does! I heard him mention his name on Wednesday on the golf course. It was just as he hooked his ball and the lake received its latest baptism. If your boss already knows God, don't you think it's all right to talk to him and ask him what kind of relationship he has with His Son? You do believe that you must be born again to get to heaven, don't you Mr. Potter?"

Pastor Prime was cooking. Mr. Potter gave a slight nod and fidgeted with his collar. He thought it was tight when he buttoned it, but it seemed tighter.

"And Mrs. Kirkland, your brother-in-law knows Jesus and he's not afraid to shout it to the world. I heard him the other day when his hammer hit the nail on his thumb instead of the one he was trying to drive into the wood.

" I hollered at him and said, 'You're right Mr. Kirkland. Jesus knows all about nails.' He must not have heard me, because he didn't answer. Were you the one who told him about Jesus, Mrs. Kirkland?"

Old Mrs. Kirkland squirmed in her pew, dusting it a little. As the second of the congregation was singled out, others slid down in their pews. They hoped they would not be next. Few would be spared. Pastor Prime's job was to save souls and he only got them once a week. Some of them he did not get that often. No one had ever slept through one of his sermons.

Pastor Prime paused for a moment and surveyed the crowd. Yes, it was a good Sunday.

Chutes And Ladders

Nancy attended a large church. Not everyone knew her. Some knew that she was a successful career woman, but one Sunday morning they found out much more about her.

Each Sunday morning someone in Nancy's church shared about how God had been working in his or her life. One day someone asked Nancy if she would be willing to speak the following week.

"Some of you know me, but few of you know who I used to be. I was married to a man who was in mid-management of a large corporation. My husband had no idea how unhappy I was. Still, we stayed together. Things changed from bad to worse the day my doctor discovered that the lump in my breast was malignant.

"My husband began to think of me as less of a woman. He started to work a lot of nights, only he was not working. To make matters a little more complicated, the small company where I worked went out of business and I was out of a job.

"My husband decided to leave me. I couldn't make ends meet. I soon found out that anyone could become homeless. Luckily, we had no children.

"Only through prayer and determination was I able to pick myself up and land on my feet. I found a job. Then I found a better job. A year or so later I started my own business."

As each person listened intently, the tears changed to smiles. But Nancy was not finished. Her story was not about herself, but about God.

"As a small child, I played Chutes And Ladders. You probably remember playing Chutes And Ladders when you were a child, but do you know that you're still playing Chutes And Ladders, only now it's for real and it's called life. Ladders can be so much fun, but chutes can take the wind out of your sails.

"No one minds another victory, climbing another ladder, but just when you're ready to climb another ladder you find yourself sliding down the chute and having to start over again. Since most people don't know how to handle chutes or ladders, let me give you some helpful advice. The way to enjoy life is to approach every chute and every ladder the same way.

"I see a few raised eyebrows, but what I say is true. Most people climb a ladder and pat themselves on the back as if to tell themselves how great they are. When those same people find themselves sliding down a chute and landing hard, they either sit there in self pity or they cry out loudly to God, as if they think He's left and gone somewhere else.

"Let me share something that may surprise some of you. You're not the only person who has ever slid down a chute. Everybody does. There's nothing wrong with sliding down the chute. There's only something wrong with staying down. Get up before someone lands on you. Jesus didn't stay in the grave, so you shouldn't stay in the pits.

"So how are you going to get up? God! God hasn't left. He's always been there and He'll continue to be there. When you find yourself at the top of the next ladder, there's Jesus Christ to help you up, and when you find yourself falling down the next chute, Jesus is there to catch you. When you decide that Jesus is there for you whether you have just climbed another ladder or fallen down another chute, you'll realize that this life is a lot more palatable. You'll be able to enjoy it, just as you did the game Chutes and Ladders you played as a kid."

As Nancy finished and turned to leave, the congregation stood and applauded. The pastor moved toward her sporting a big grin and a warm hug.

As the applause died down, the pastor approached the microphone and shared a few short words. "The victory is won. My sermon can wait until next Sunday."